Triptych: Choices: Three Novellas

In the arts, a triptych is defined as "a set of three associated artistic, literary, or musical works intended to be appreciated together." Such is this new offering by acclaimed author, Annabel Thomas, who weaves together stories from rural Ohio, some set in the not-so-distant past, others harking back to a simpler time in America.

Thomas deftly weaves together three apparently disparate stories into a cohesive tale of humanity with living characters. A young woman's love and lust for a beautiful but seemingly unreachable man, the ebbing sexual life between a geriatric couple whose love remains hopeful, and a lone woman wandering an airport on a fateful day for America's race for Space, all beautifully coalesce with bits of literature, religion, humor, memory, hope, and passion.

In answer to the incessant question posed by Addie's unhappy mother: "What exactly is the point?" we can learn through the lives of these characters that, in the face of being grounded, we continue to seek and will always find within ourselves some defiance of gravity. For in the end, that redundant image of loss we are offered daily in the modern world "seems not so much to show the destruction...as to praise the valiant, the determined, unceasing effort of the launch."

~Christina Lovin, author of *Echo: Poems* and *God of Sparrows*

Othe Books by Annabel Thomas

The Phototropic Woman, University of Iowa Press, 1981.
A Well of Living Water, novella in *Human Anatomy: Three Fictions,*
        Bottom Dog Press, 1993.
Knucklebones, Helicon Nine Editions, 1995.
Blood Feud, University of Tennessee Press, 1998.
Stone Man Mountain, University of Tennessee Press, 2002.

Bottom Dog Press

Choices

Three Novellas

Annabel Thomas

Appalachian Writing Series
Bottom Dog Press
Huron, Ohio

Credits
General Editor Larry Smith
Editor & Introduction: Elizabeth Lantz
Cover art by J. Robert Taylor
from Wisconsin Historical Society
Cover Design by Susanna Sharp-Schwacke

Acknowledgments

"Tuesday at the Airport," previously published
as"Sunday at the Airport' originally appeared in
The Ohio Review, No. 57, Spring 1998.

Contents

Dedication

For Elizabeth
Without your help there would be no book.

Introduction
by Elizabeth Lantz

Some utter honesty and uniqueness of character makes a person who he is. If there's a spiritual dimension to us, then that's the point of connection. I think our spiritual part involves love of other people, compassion, empathy for our fellows. It's the source of the meaning of life in a way not entirely clear to me, and I guess I write stories to try to figure out what this is all about. So writes my mother, Annabel Thomas, to explain what motivates her work.

From the time I left home for college, we have maintained a continual written correspondence. Like Addie's mother in "Tuesday at the Airport," she has always been driven to find out what life is about. And it's through her writing that she finds answers:

All my life I've lived on two levels. Ordinary everyday happenings and then it's as if a great intense light switches on, and I see the same things but see their real meanings or see connections and dimensions with a breathtaking clarity. But it only comes in bits and snatches, and all the rest of the time I wander around lost and longing for it and trying by various means to tear the blinders off my eyes.

Writing well causes the blinders to fall off. Also, reading: *If I ever get to thinking the world is an awful place, all I have to do is dive into literature and I feel bursting with hope and joy. I wish I could read every good book that was ever written and learn all about everything there is to know.*

In "Dorsey and the Amishman," the choices made by a young couple reveal how *all people are creating themselves, like artists create a work of art, by what their intuition chooses to remember and what symbols their minds make of it.*

When I read "The Lost Book" for the first time, I recognized a version of my parents. Upon reaching the empty nest stage of life, my mother wrote:

Being alone again with my husband is wonderful! I would rather be alone with him than in any other state of being. It's like being in a state of grace. It's like drinking on and on from a well that quenches, satisfies you soul. It's as if we've always been having this deep, serious, vital, wordless intent, breathlessly absorbing conversation and behind and between and amongst everything else we do, it goes on.

My father was always my mother's greatest fan. He kept the family posted on her projects and progress. In one letter, she confessed:

The other day I ran my dryer for 40 minutes without any clothes in it. Then I went out and tried for quite a long time to start the car by pushing determinedly on the brake pedal. I told Father about these two things, and he beamed and said, "You must be writing well."

On the other hand, she bemoaned her suffering when she faced writer's block. Over the years, her correspondence was peppered with references to this syndrome:

I write to you from the slough of despond. I don't feel like whacking off my ear. But close to it, close.

Or:

I'm down in a crevice I can't climb out of. I have all these disconnected notes and ideas and a character that keeps hiding behind rocks and peeping out at me.

She has never stopped seeking out the characters who speak to her. She has never stopped hearing their voices. And she has never stopped sharing them with me and the world.

I remember a story in which a little boy said to his grandfather, "Did you ever see God?" and the old man replied, "It's getting any more so I can't see anything but God." I keep now seeing these glimpses of the unchanging, this brief touching of fingertips with perfect love, everywhere, in every thing. Especially in all kinds of art. In all kinds of human relationships.

Dorsey and the Amishman

Dorsey's favorite memories were of visits to the farm where her father spent his boyhood. She'd sat in the kitchen beside a wood-burning stove while her great-aunts quilted on a frame and conversed in a strange tongue. The older generation of Bendlers spoke German.

When the great aunts died, the farm was sold so that, at last, there was nothing left of it in Dorsey's life except these memories. After her mama left, in her unhappiness Dorsey developed a dream life in which she and Papa returned to the farm. In this secret world she sat with him beside the wood-burning stove, quilting and (quite miraculously) speaking with him in the German language. Back when the three of them were still a family, her papa, Logan, had often talked of re-visiting the home farm but they never did. Mama had no interest in it. She wished to travel to far-off places, but they never did that, either. In the end, Mama subscribed to the *National Geographic* instead.

One day Mama had opened a *Geographic* and showed Dorsey pictures of the Le Brea Tar Pits. There they lay, black and imponderable, in them the remains of prehistoric bears, saber-toothed tigers, giant wolves, llamas, camels, horses, enormous ground sloths, all preserved in layers of oil and tar.

The animals had been sucked under as they drank from a shallow pool that covered the sticky asphalt bog. Dorsey stared at the pictures, rubbing across them with the tips of her fingers.

"When I'm grown up, I'll go to Hancock Park in Los Angeles," Dorsey said, "and look at the trapped animals."

"Look at me," Dorsey's mother Iva told her. "It's the same thing as looking at them."

A week later, she left. When Dorsey and her papa got up on a Monday morning, they found Iva had packed her bags and gone.

Although Dorsey was only eight, she missed her mother less than one would imagine. She was closer to her papa because, even when Iva was there, she'd seemed to be in another place, doing another thing: singing songs.

Before she married, she'd been a vocalist with a dance orchestra. This was in the era of the big bands. She'd imagined herself singing with Jimmy and Tommy Dorsey although she never made it that big. She'd nicknamed her daughter "Dorsey," as a way of holding onto her dream. Dorsey's real name was Ursula.

Dorsey's papa, Logan Bendler, wrote books. Travel pamphlets and county histories containing anecdotes out of the past and directions for locating battle sites, the homes of early settlers and monuments put up to honor the notable dead. Down the years Iva had helped him with his research and typed and edited his manuscripts. When Iva departed, the job fell to Dorsey. It took up most of her free time.

Logan also wrote a series called *Everyman's Biographies of Great Writers*. These small books were his real passion. He had done George Eliot, Walter Scott, Thackery, Dickens, Hardy and Meredith. The year Iva left, he began on D. H. Lawrence, his favorite. It was years later, after her father had begun to show the first signs of Parkinson's, that Dorsey, sorting through his papers, came across the Lawrence biography still unfinished.

The summer after Iva left, Dorsey went to camp. Logan said he'd rather she stayed home, but the money had been paid and couldn't be refunded and so, in the end, she went.

The children swam and boated and learned crafts. Dorsey signed up for weaving. She made a scarf of blue and white wool using a large wooden hand loom. She strung the blue threads lengthwise in rows on the frame, very close together, then laced the white yarn in crosswise, using the shuttle. She raised and lowered the lengthwise threads with her fingers to let the shuttle pass under and over them.

This was the ancient way of weaving. Begun in the New Stone Age, it grew into a fine art in Egypt and Persia. In China and India, Greece and Rome. The instructor showed pictures of tapestries made in Arras in Flanders in the fourteen hundreds.

These pictures took Dorsey's breath away.

When she returned home, all she cared to talk about was weaving cloth. Nothing before in her life had given her such pleasure.

During the remaining years she lived with her papa in Tapp City, Dorsey sometimes woke in the night and knew she had been weaving. Felt, in the muscles of her shoulders and arms, a lacing rhythm and, across her fingerpads, the bite of threads.

After they moved to the country, these dreams stopped, but only for a while.

— 2 —

Once the arrow flies, only the empty bow is left, a thing without character or purpose. This is how Dorsey thought about the possibility of her father's death. Papa was the arrow; she was the bow.

Parkinson's Disease, the doctors said, was incurable. A growing rigidity. An increasingly fixed facial expression. Escalating difficulties in speech, chewing and swallowing. First, a shuffling gate. Then a cane. Then a walker. And last, a wheelchair. On the other hand, Papa might continue on for many years. He might die of another disease altogether.

The diagnosis made them examine how they were living their lives.

"I want to leave Tapp City," Logan told his daughter. "I want to look out my windows and see farmland once again."

By moving to the country, Logan Bendler hoped to return somehow to his younger days when he'd helped operate a dairy and when, as the only boy in a family of females, he'd been coddled and spoiled by his mother, his grandmother, his sisters and his aunts.

Even after he left the farm, these sorts of women were in his life. Women who comforted him and smoothed his way. Without them he was lonely, even undone. He was weaker than anyone imagined. Not so competent nor so creative as he seemed. He needed constant shoring up.

Still, if one woman departed, another always came to take her place. And this was acceptable since, if the truth were known, all women, even his young wife Iva, even his daughter Ursula, seemed to him non-specific in their similarity. To Logan, women were interchangeable.

Only when he felt the Parkinson's stiffening his sinews, did his Ursula gain a measure of uniqueness since he came to believe he could place her between himself and the ailment that gnawed at him and so conquer it and survive.

Dorsey was seventeen when she and her father moved from Tapp City to the village of Captina. Logan had just turned sixty. The year was 1972. Logan's only regret was that he must give up his weekly games of golf.

Their house, clapboarded, two-storied, sat on the hamlet's west edge. They had a large garden space and, behind the toolshed, a woodlot. When they took possession, the fields around Captina hung heavy with abundant harvest.

After the move, Dorsey found herself, for a time, thrown on her own devices. Logan was busy conferring with plumbers and electricians, painters and roofers. The house needed many repairs.

A number of young people lived in Captina. Boys and girls who were friendly and full of fun. Soon Dorsey swam with them in the village pool, roller-skated, danced, attended movies. She went where she wanted to go.

*

One evening when Dorsey was away from home, and during a pause in the work on the kitchen, Logan walked alone out across the backyard. He used a cane now, and what with

the uneven ground, he must put his feet down very carefully.
It took him a good twenty minutes to make his way to the
yard's edge. Looking to the west he saw the sun enlarged and
flushed by its nearness to the horizon.

All the rolling land in the valley lay dappled and softened in its strange rosy light. Logan saw farmyards and salt box
houses. He saw barns with open lofts and hay being forked in.
Beyond the barns, spotted cattle grazed in clover meadows.

Logan told himself he knew these cattle. Knew the
warmth in the hollows of their sides, knew their sweet breath,
the roll of their heavy bones and the feel of their milk-distend-
ed udders.

Looking beyond the cattle, up across the fields, of
a sudden he seemed to see a number of women kneeling in
prayer. It was a trick of the sunset. As the red light faded, the
shapes resumed their true identity as corn shocks.

And now on the road below he saw a horse-drawn buggy. And about the barns, farmers and farmers' wives dressed in
the old way doing chores done in his boyhood.

As he made his way back to the house and feeling
light-headed, Logan told himself that, in some mysterious way,
things past and gone were come again.

— 3 —

When Menno first saw her, she was playing volleyball
on a sand court beside the village swimming pool. She wore
orange and blue shorts and a green muscle shirt over her swimsuit. When she hit the ball, flowered latex peeped through.
Her tanned arms, her slim, straight legs, flickered in the sun.
Bright-colored she was, with tiny bones.

Her hair was shoulder length and loose, the way Outsider girls wore it now. As she moved, it rose and fell, wing-like,
against her shoulders. Flitting here, flitting there, she seemed
light as a bird whereas Menno felt earthbound. Felt stuck to
the dirt by his thick shoes, heavy as anvils.

A car parked beside the court had its doors open. Its radio was blaring unclean music, the volume turned up as high as it would go.

Sometimes a ball bounced out of play. Waiting for someone to retrieve it, she grabbed up a fistful of sand and let it run through her fingers while her glance slid here and there marking, he supposed, which boys were watching her, asking herself, the way girls do, *Is he the one?*

All at once, in spite of himself, Menno thought, *Let it be me!*

Then he turned away, his face draining of color. He knew well enough when the Devil had made a grab at him.

The first glimpse Dorsey had of Menno, she thought he resembled Hans Brinker. Or the Dutch boy in housepaint ads. Those floppy clothes, that haircut, that solemn face.

The way he turned his head as he drove his buggy past, his wide, unblinking eyes fastened on her, made her want to kick sand at him. Or rip off her clothes and really give him something to stare at. She made a face at him, and he looked away.

To him it was natural that he should watch her, since she was like a bird. Birdwatching was one of the few recreations he was allowed, *they* were allowed, he and the other young people of his sect. It was granted to them to own binoculars and birding books. Each spring they rode a bus up to the lake to see the warblers pass through on their way to their breeding ground in Michigan.

These birds clustered, twittering and calling, in trees and bushes along the shore seeming to work up the nerve to fly off across the blue-gray expanse of Lake Erie. Menno sensed the same feeling in the girl. That she was working up her nerve. For what he couldn't say.

He never approached her. To do so would have been improper, both because she was an Outsider and because the plans for his wedding were more or less set. The commitment was a secret one but settled all the same between the two of them. One day soon, the parents of his future bride would be told and would give their consent. The deacon would inform the bishop. His mother would tell him, "You will learn to love her."

Naomi Muller was blue-eyed and flaxen-haired. They had known each other all their lives. Not one of the People would be surprised when the bans were given out.

"She'll make you a good wife," his brothers would tell him. "She's a hard-worker and will bring with her a fine dowery." He had never courted anyone else.

However, it was also true that Menno Yoder had lived his life haunted by an odd vision: that of an unknown girl with shadows in her eyes. Layer on layer of darkness overlapped like leaves.

For months at a time, he would be free of her only to wake one morning knowing she'd been with him during the night.

What this meant he couldn't imagine. Some sort of omen, perhaps. Like being born with a caul.

He never told anyone. Yet, because of this strange visitation, he felt himself different from the other men. From his younger brothers and his father and his uncles. His thoughts were different. And his yearnings. For instance, this very evening he was loafing about in a worldly place where none of the People would come or if they came, would not stay. His ears rang with the wild music bursting out its windows: music that surely blackened the soul.

This building, containing a roller-skating rink, stood half a mile from Captina, distanced from the village proper like a bordello.

He was here because Dorsey was here. He'd followed her as she walked out from town with a bunch of Captina girls.

He'd never been drawn to an Outsider girl before. At least not to one particular girl. None of the boys could help looking at the bare skin these girls showed. At their knees and thighs and at their dimpled shoulders. And at the wonder of their masses of free-swinging hair.

They stared at the Outsider girls in the same way they stared at the cars the Worlds drove. They wanted to touch them in almost the same way. But wanting and doing were different things. They had grown up with temptation all around them. They knew how to deal with it. "Be not conformed to this world," they had been told. "Be not unequally yoked together with unbelievers." "What communion hath light and darkness?"

Of course, a few of the boys "went high" now and again. Left the settlement and disappeared into the world. Some came back after a while. Shem, Menno's oldest brother, had done that.

"I won't think about Shem," Menno said out loud, so that a woman passing by turned her head and looked at him. Menno felt rattled and thought he would go back to the store where his buggy was tied. But just then the doors were flung open and he looked through and saw her. She was skimming over the floor while about her head danced a thousand silver spackles like the shattered pieces of a star.

*

For pure cheekiness, he took the prize! Wherever she went, there he came after her, staring at her out of those Hans Brinker eyes. Even her friends noticed.

"There's your Amishman," her friends said.

He made them giggle with his barndoor pants and his great flat-topped hat. He never took it off. Dorsey wondered what his hair looked like underneath. All she could see was the blonde fringe around his earlobes. His chin was pink and smooth.

"His father's a shelf-maker," her friends told her. "He builds cabinets out of wood. He and his brothers are shelf-makers, too. When he gets married, he'll grow a beard," they told her. "Right now, he's single. He's saving himself for you."

To be teased about such a one: the nuisance! He drove her crazy. Smiling seemed beyond him. It was as if his face might crack and fall on the floor at his feet.

Above Dorsey's head the great mirror-ball turned, and she and all the other skaters went around and around until she couldn't feel her feet.

Every time she glimpsed the soda pop machine, she turned her head so as not to see him standing next to it. The recorded music from the loudspeaker drowned out all other sound except for the wordless hissing of the skate wheels.

Two of her girlfriends caught hold of her hands and they went around, three together. Then it was time to leave because the owners were blinking the lights.

Sitting on a bench unlacing her skates, she forgot about him. When she looked up, there he stood, an arm's length off, staring.

Out of nowhere she thought, *He's got Papa's eyes!* and a tingling went up the back of her neck. It was the first time she'd brought the two of them together in her thoughts.

— 4 —

Shortly after he moved to Captina, it became clear that Logan Bendler's disease was progressing rather faster than the doctors had expected. The medicine he took wasn't helping. Both sides of his body were affected. Walking, he was increasingly unsteady. He moved more and more cautiously, afraid of tumbling down. The right-hand tremor took the form of pin-rolling, a continual rubbing of forefinger against thumb. He was commencing, perhaps, to see the world in a distorted way, for he wrote now in a cramped hand all at one corner of the paper.

However, in spite of his stiffening hands, he outlined an ambitious and detailed history of Knox County, Ohio, where they now lived, and began to occupy Dorsey's time with ordering books, verifying facts and typing out notes.

She welcomed the work. She had been feeling slack and becalmed. Now she billowed out with energetic activity.

In addition to the county history, Logan proposed to spend his evenings re-reading Lawrence in preparation for going forward with the biography. He began with the book he, alone of Lawrence scholars, placed above the others, *Sons and Lovers*. On finishing it, he said, "When I'm gone, Ursula, scatter my ashes over Lawrence's grave in New Mexico." So that at once, in her mind's eye, she saw his lovely, slender body fallen to cinders. "And if I haven't finished his biography," Logan continued, "then you must finish it for me."

But she left the room and wouldn't come back until her papa had ceased speaking of such things.

While Logan was reading, Dorsey busied herself with hooking a rag rug to lay upon the hearth.

The grandmother of one of her Captina girlfriends instructed her on how it should be done. Dorsey had brought a box of old clothes from Tapp City, intending to use them as cleaning rags: Logan's worn-out shirts and trousers, her own outgrown skirts and blouses, a few garments her mother had left behind. Now each evening she sat in a pool of lamplight tearing these fabrics carefully in the way she'd been taught.

"You take the ends of old things," the grandmother had explained, "and out of them you make the beginning of something new."

Tearing Iva's dresses, Dorsey wondered, as she'd often done before, where her mother had gone. There were times she felt she knew. Times she seemed to hear her mama speaking to her inside her head.

I went looking for the ballrooms, Iva said and Dorsey understood that she meant The Palladium, the Steel Pier, the Indian Roof, the Palamar, Roseland, the Glenn Allen Casino. All those gorgeous places she'd always told about. "The musicians signed their names on the walls," Iva had used to say. And so, Dorsey supposed she'd gone to read their names.

She had told how colored lights hung from the ceilings and the bands played on a raised platform while dancing couples filled the floors. How the band members, wearing white coats, stood in painted boxes and blew on saxophones and trombones and trumpets. Only the vocalist was free to walk about singing into a hand mike, moving to the music.

When Dorsey told Papa her speculations, Papa had said, "She never sang with a band good enough to play those places. If she went there now," he said, "she'd find most of them closed or torn down. The sort of music she knew how to sing, is long gone."

*

Menno Yoder stepped into the house on the west edge of Captina where his father and two of his brothers were measuring heights and widths. He seldom went into the Worlds' homes. His part of the cabinetmaking was done in the shop. He'd come because he wanted to see where she lived.

Once he was in the house, he couldn't help but stare. Thick drapes and heavy curtains fell in folds over the windows, coloring the light. The floors lay buried under carpet that muffled his footsteps like moss. The walls were pasted with flowered paper and hung with ornaments and pictures in such a profusion of shapes and hues they hurt his eyes. A clutter of books and lamps, statuettes of marble and bronze together with little painted dishes were scattered over tables and sideboard.

The crippled writer, leaning on his cane, followed Menno into the kitchen. He and Menno's father discussed hinges. Where the cabinets should be placed and how many would be needed and the number of shelves each should contain.

She's gone swimming, Menno thought. *Or she's out riding her bicycle. You're not going to see her*, he told himself, and an ache like the rasp of a file played along his ribs.

Then Dorsey came into the kitchen. Her hands were full of papers. She said to her father, "How should I do this?" And the World, Logan Bendler, told her how.

She kept her chin tucked down and didn't look at Menno or at his father or his brothers.

When the measuring was completed, the computations were written down. Just before Menno and his father and his brothers departed, Menno, with a surreptitious fling, sent his tape measure scooting under a chair.

While his father and brothers waited for him in the buggy, he turned back into the unclean house and, on his way to retrieve the tape, managed to pass by the room where Dorsey was working. He looked at her in her bondage.

The thought that came into his head was this: *She is like the martyrs.*

This recognition startled him and, in some subtle way, changed him. Before this thought, he'd seen Dorsey in one way. Ever afterward he saw her in another.

*

Several weeks later when Menno, his father, and his brothers returned to fit the finished cabinets to the walls and fasten them in place, Menno arranged to catch Dorsey by herself in her vegetable garden. Without greeting or nod, almost without looking at her, he asked her to go with him the next day to his cousin's wedding. Then he held his breath.

She stood silent before him a long time. He saw that she wanted to be rid of him and at the same time longed to attend the wedding.

"All right," she said at last. "I'll meet you at your place. Tell me how to get there."

He understood that she didn't want her friends to see her riding by his side in his bachelor buggy.

*

On the appointed day, she peddled her bicycle to his house and traveled to the location of the wedding in the Yoder family carriage. His sisters and brothers were polite to her but pulled away from her in hidden ways so as not to be contaminated by her worldliness

The wedding rites were mysterious. Dorsey saw them as being like the secret initiations of lodges: the Masons or the Odd Fellows or the Elks. A great deal of what went on was in German.

The preaching and the praying lasted more than three hours. Dorsey's muscles hurt from sitting so long on a backless wooden bench.

The hymns were startling. Overpowering. They were sung in unison and their volume shook the walls and pounded the ceiling. The German words were guttural and electrifying.

When the first sermon began, the men removed their hats and she saw Menno's hair. It shone in the strong light coming through a bare window. It lay on his head straight and smooth and hung like a sheet of polished brass down the back of his neck.

The men and boys sat in one place, the women and girls in another. Everyone, even the bride and groom, wore plain colored clothes. In her bright print dress, Dorsey felt like a butterfly wandered in amongst dark trees.

During the first hymns, they watched the bride and groom climb to an upstairs room to be instructed, by the bishop and the deacons, how to live a proper married life.

As soon as Naomi sat down beside her, Dorsey understood that some sort of bond existed between this girl and Menno. It was clear in the way Naomi looked at her. This discovery also seemed part of the strange riddle that was the wedding.

After the joining, everyone traveled to the bride's home where a meal was set out. At the food-filled tables, the men sat on one side, the women on the other. Silent prayers were offered. The bride and groom were served first. As they ate, the people told jokes on the bride and groom. The air was full of laughter.

Dozens of children ran about. The women talked together of child-rearing, boiling down soap and apple butter, working up pickles, tending poultry. The men spoke to other men of the seasons. Of plowing and planting and harvest. Barn-building and horse-swapping.

Before they left the tables, more prayers were said and more hymns sung.

Out in the barn, where the young people played "Skip to My Lou" and "There Goes Topsy Through the Window," Menno had many different partners. Sometimes he had Naomi. Yet whenever Dorsey passed by, he felt something like the pull plants feel toward the sun. Wherever she went, his glance followed her.

It seemed to him again that she was like the martyrs. Full of suffering. Full of a deep loneliness that had to do, he believed, with the World, Logan Bendler. Looking in her eyes, he believed he saw her soul weeping.

Yet, in the "Six-Handed Reel," she was giddy and gay. Her face grew crimson from the effort of the dance. She was good at it. She footed it sure and light. Every time he touched her arm, he felt that her flesh burnt him.

She was different from his sisters. She seemed, in some strange way, to float through the pattern of the reel. He was amazed, thinking that, in the end, it would not hold her. That she would pass up and away and out of his sight. He kept expecting to see her rise and go.

After the games, standing in the bride's front yard, Dorsey watched Menno and other of the young bachelors lift the groom off his feet and toss him over a picket fence into the arms of the married men. And understood his situation was forever changed.

All the way home, riding her bicycle into the deepening twilight, Dorsey fancied she heard a rustling behind her on the road, a whispering of voices that was like blowing leaves. *"We know well who we are,"* the voices seemed to murmur. *"We are the Amish."*

You are the Amish, agreed Ursula. *But who am I?*

The voices gave no answer to her question.

— 5 —

"Come here, dearest boy," Logan's mother had said so long ago. She lifted him, a little child, onto her lap and fed him scrapings from an apple, since his milk teeth were bad. They had come in already decayed, it almost seemed. He couldn't bear hard chewing nor sweetness. Nor hot nor cold.

Sitting on his mam's knee, Logan had watched the miners walking home swinging their empty lunch pails, some of them talking, one to another, some of them singing.

His father, black as a hobgoblin, turned in at the gate.

His mam hugged Logan close. "You'll never go down-mine," she said. "Not you."

In a year's time his dad was dead, smothered in a cave-in, and the family moved to Grandma Bendler's farm where his uncles scythed hay in the blinding sun and where he began to make up poems.

When they read these poems, his aunts and his granny started to save their money to send him to the university. And so, as his mam had said, he escaped the mines.

Yet, often here in Captina, Logan woke in the dark and, for a time, believed he was underground. He felt the earth with its seams of coal squeeze him until his muscles stiffened and his breath fought to find a clear way in and out of his lungs.

Then he saw, perhaps, a star framed in a window or heard a dog bark and knew that air was about him, not earth. And, gripping the headboard, he would turn on his side and call for Ursula who came bringing him a glass of fresh-brewed tea.

At the beginning of the first winter in the new place, a large white cat attached itself to Logan. It wouldn't be driven away. It demanded food and shelter and stroking. It lay at its ease across the hearth rug or, more often, draped itself on Logan's back while he sat at his desk, writing.

As snow piled up outside, the cat took on weight and became even more immobile. Only the tip of its tail twitched or, now and again, its eyes opened exceedingly wide as if it watched for a signal to be given.

Logan grew very fond of the white cat. He was comforted by its weight along his shoulders. He called it "Toby" after a tom he'd known long ago on his Grandma Bendler's farm.

*

Every evening now, before bed, Dorsey gave her papa a massage with sweet-scented oil. A deep, vigorous rub. He had hot baths and heat lamp and medications.

For a long time, she continued to see him as he was before the Parkinson's, her beautiful papa, sleek and rounded and smiling, graceful of body, quick of mind and eye, of hand and foot, his voice deep and resonate as a beating drum.

Then one twilight, gazing, dreamy and unaware, from the kitchen window into the vegetable garden, she thought, *Who is that misshapen elf?* Understanding almost at once that it was Logan, she burst into tears.

Often now he used a walker. Without it, he got off balance and took quick little steps, almost running, to keep himself from pitching forward. Sometimes he froze in place and must be helped to start on again.

Still, he got about for the most part on his own and, in the evenings, read aloud to Dorsey from *Sons and Lovers,* the parts about Morel, the father, working in the coal mines, and, from *The Rainbow,* the descriptions of the farmhouse with the barn attached and the people caring for their animals in winter.

He did the same bits over and over, reading in a low-pitched monotone.

Out of curiosity, Dorsey finished *The Rainbow,* since her name came from its pages, and went on to *Women in Love* in which Ursula breaks with her past and reaches out for a new beginning. She read out loud to Logan the famous bit about man and wife as two stars, joined by a gravity-like pull, yet separate. However, he closed the book as it lay in her lap and began to talk of other things.

Dorsey's typing consisted of copying out Logan's long-hand which became increasingly hard to decipher. Now and again her mind wandered so that her hands lay idle on the keys and, instead of the manuscript before her, she re-examined sights she'd witnessed during the day.

Sometimes she saw the Amish as they were in winter. The barns and houses topped with snow. The smooth, pale fields crisscrossed by the marks of cows' feet, the roads scored by the runners of sleighs and sleds. Or a funeral procession going up the hill beyond Menno's house. A row of buggies, ebony against the marble-white earth, mounting to the crest of the hill where gravestones, all of a size, poked thorough the drifts like finger bones.

Or she saw, instead of present things, past ones in other places. She recalled the recorded sounds of saxophones and clarinets, trombones and cornets and drums embedded in the hiss of a phonograph needle as it rode the groove around and around.

In her mind's eye Mama lay on the couch in Tapp City, listening, smoke from her cigarette veiling her face. Or Mama swayed about the room, singing to the records, her voice flaring like the horns.

"Fabulous Dorsey!" She heard her mother's voice call her once again. "Because," Mama said, "you will make something of your own someday. Something original, like Swing."

Dorsey had to admit, however, that the person most often in her mind was Menno. Often since the wedding, they'd arranged to meet in Captina. While the good weather held, they walked about the streets or else out through the fields to the west. At first, conversation was difficult. Before long, however, they found themselves chattering to one another about their earlier lives and about their present thoughts.

*

When the temperature had stayed below zero for a long enough time, Menno and his brothers and the other men began work on the ponds. Thirty men drove in ten wagons. They cut the ice into 200-pound blocks and packed it in sawdust and in straw.

Even through his knitted gloves, the blue-white, slippery chunks froze Menno's fingers. They were like pieces of the winter season itself which, become tactile, stung and stiffened his flesh.

Seeing the black water, robbed of its cover, and lying atremble in the wind, he imagined the fishes, hanging at pond's bottom sluggish with dreams of the lost summer.

When all the blocks were stored in the ice shed, Menno and his father and his brothers busied themselves with mending harness and, in the shop, with building cupboards. As the winter went on, they put new handles to the plow and a new axle to the wagon, patched the buggy tops and sharpened the hoes, the scythes and the sickles.

Once, at bedtime, when Menno went out to check on the horses, he saw Captina sending a glow up the dark night and pictured Dorsey in her house at the village edge caring for the sick World, Logan Bendler.

Overhead the stars and planets appeared in their patterns and he thought that, surely, all such were set in their places by the hand of God. And he thought that, perhaps, once He'd set them, these patterns hampered Him in ways similar to the ways patterns of their own making now and again hampered men.

The horses whickered to Menno from their stalls. Shifting their ponderous weight, they raised their great heads, blotting out the rafters. They blew their warm breath into the hollow of his neck, glad that he'd come.

He checked their drinking water and their hay and grain, then, leaning his head against one of the huge pulling-collars that hung on pegs along the wall, he sighed and closed his eyes.

Menno shared a bedroom with his brothers. In order to think of Dorsey with proper concentration, he must come to the barn. The lantern flickered and he trimmed the wick. The little blue and yellow flame steadied and increased.

Although he'd entered the barn to be alone, yet he was not alone. His brother Shem was, as always, with him. Here in the horse-scented, hay-sweet dark, Shem, uninvited, kept him company.

Not Shem himself, of course, for he was dead. It was his brother's presence or perhaps only his memory that remained in the place where he had breathed his last, where the beam he'd used to hang himself still marked the floor with its shadow.

Most generally, Menno could push Shem away and think only of Dorsey. He did this now, even though a loop of harness dangled down the wall just as it had on that earlier night, handy to Shem's purpose.

After a time, Menno heard a step on the path outside. Addie, the sister nearest him in age, came into the barn, wrapped in a shawl. She was expecting a child. All of her was filled full and rounded: her breasts, her belly, her face. She knelt in the corner where the apples were buried and secured one for herself and one for Zoar, her husband.

"The rest are gone to bed," she told him. "You'd best come to the stove and not be lingering out here doting on Naomi!"

He picked up the lantern and followed her to the house, surprised at what she knew, relieved at what she didn't.

— 6 —

On a day in early spring, Dorsey saw Menno walking over the field below the woodlot. He was picking up rocks. Later, she saw him plowing the field with a five-horse hitch.

He wore a straw hat with a flat brim and, fastened to his pants, wide blue suspenders.

She'd scarce had a sight of him since the ice-cutting began. She knew he was busy with winter chores. She'd grown uneasy, however, since she couldn't help wondering if, perhaps, he and Naomi had published their bans.

She watched him lay each new row along the old, straight and true across the field like lines on ruled paper. Back and forth he went, opening the earth to the seed as this had been done in her papa's boyhood. Mewing like kittens, two killdeers flew low over the furrows, seeking a nesting place.

Along the edges of the turned ground the tree branches with their small spring leaves rose and fell like the arms of swimmers. The warm wind lifted her hair and brushed her cheeks. Menno looked up and, seeing her at the top of the slope, raised his hand. And she raised hers.

When the horses came along the side of the field nearest her, Menno stopped them and shouted up to her. She walked a ways toward him before she understood.

"Meet me here this time tomorrow," Menno shouted. "Come and help me plant trees."

*

The next afternoon Dorsey and Menno set sycamores in the swales and along the creek. In the sunny uplands, they planted walnut seedlings.

It had rained in the night and was threatening to rain again. Their spades made sucking noises, coming out. They stuck the hair-fine roots into the holes and covered them with earth, tamping it with the backs of their spades.

The new trees seemed quickly at home. Once Dorsey accidentally pulled out a just-planted seedling and found an earthworm already clinging to its roots.

They arranged the trees in open spaces on a hillside where older trees had been cut down.

"We plant," explained Menno, "so that there may always be trees. So that there will always be lumber for cabinets and for barns and logs for cooking and for heating."

What Dorsey thought was this: *You are a tree yourself: rooted in the old ways.*

Menno showed her a twist of hair caught on a briar, white and kinky as sheep's wool. "From the tail of a deer," he said. Small two-toed prints patterned the wet ground. The tracks, he said, were quite fresh, probably a doe's.

"I wish I'd seen her!"

"She's gone out of the woods by now."

"If we climbed a tree, we might see her cross the fields."

Dorsey ran in amongst the older trees, looking for one easy to climb. Menno turned away, keeping a secret: if he found himself very far off the ground, his stomach flopped and quivered.

Dorsey, beginning to scramble up a pin oak, called impatiently, "Come on! Come on!"

Menno walked slowly to the oak and stood peering up the way she'd gone. He saw her knees, her calves, then the bottoms of her shoes disappearing amongst the leaves.

He stood a while, staring up. Then, gripping a lower limb, he swung his body off the ground. High up, where the branches thinned out, he wrapped his legs around the trunk and shinnied up it. A branch scraped off his hat. Looking down he dizzily beheld the ground dropping away. His breath came in short gasps. Sweat started everywhere on his skin.

Far above him, Dorsey gazed out across the distant fields. She saw a darkness in a fence corner that could be a deer or could be only the shadow cast by a bush.

Menno had never been so far above the earth. Fear squeezed his chest. Yet he was also thrilled to be where birds lived and high breezes blew. Above him she swung out, an elbow hooked around the trunk, the other arm angling down toward the field, a finger pointing.

As a schoolboy, Menno had learned to juggle pears. He felt now that he rose like the pears, curved through the air, then dropped. It was a sensation caused by a sudden increase in the wind, swaying the treetops. Without looking into the field, he started to climb down.

As they descended, a light rain began. Moist leaves slid across Menno's skin like licking tongues. The branches became treacherously slick so that his fingers slipped, and he dropped with a yell, alternately catching himself back and losing hold. He plummeted the last five feet and lay on the ground, the breath knocked out of him.

When he opened his eyes, Dorsey was bending over him. Her hair hung in his face, tickling his nose. Her face so close, her eyes enormous.

Menno got to his feet, bruised and chagrined.

Meanwhile the rain pelted down. They ran under the dripping trees. In the hillside, Menno showed Dorsey a small cave. They squeezed into it, their faces toward the narrow mouth.

It was an extremely tight fit. Pressed together, hip and thigh, they warmed one another. Menno might have embraced her if his arms hadn't been flattened beneath his chest. Dorsey, listening to his breathing, felt plainly that he might have.

A gust of rain blew into the cave wetting their faces. She saw his damp hair stuck to his skull, looking, she thought, as her papa's had looked these past few weeks when he'd had night sweats. Of a sudden she felt a great wrench of sadness.

This feeling came, she thought, because of Papa. Or because she had missed seeing the wild doe. Or perhaps it was due only to the dark sky which seemed of a sudden akin to the half-light down open graves.

On the other hand, the wind's steady beat in the branches put her in mind of the Amish hymns so that she said to Menno, "Why were the wedding songs sung in German?"

He explained that his German-speaking forebears had created the hymns in the 16th century. "Those of our ancestors persecuted for not recanting their faith," he listed. "Those publicly burned and garroted, beheaded, drowned and maimed. Nearly a thousand died. The hymns told the suffering and loneliness of the persecuted.

"And yet," Menno said, "the chorales are triumphant. They make us try to live our lives as they lived theirs, and so to triumph over sin and over those who are unclean."

In the close quarters of the cave opening, Dorsey turned her face to his. "Why do you call me unclean?" she asked him. "I bathe the same as you."

"Because you're of the World."

"So are you. So is everyone."

"We are not of the World," he said. "We are of the Everlasting."

Dorsey felt as she did at the roller rink when she skated too fast, only instead of her feet losing their purchase, it was her mind. She wriggled from the cave into the rain. He followed her and they stood facing one another.

Dorsey said, "You die just as we do."

As Menno tried to explain, he felt the rain fasten strands of his hair across his mouth as if to silence him. "Our ways don't change," he told her, "and so we are eternal." Even an English girl must understand this. He stared at her helplessly through the wall of the downpour. Her parted lips were pink and wet as dewy roses.

He thought of the martyrs, of their gifts and their demands and of the *Ordnung*, the rules by which the People conducted their lives. He thought how without these he'd be less holy but also less burdened, less constricted.

She stared at him, her brows drawn together, repeating, "We all die."

He understood it was a personal thing with her. That she wanted to stop this happening but lacked the knowledge.

She looked at him expectantly as if he might hand her directions for putting an end to death as he might give her the plans for building a cabinet.

Without his hat, Menno's head felt exposed. His brain felt water-logged. For a while he was silent. Then he gave her, in English, the sayings he had heard spoken in German by bishops and ministers and deacons.

"Get right with God," Menno declaimed. "Let the young brethren be as the old brethren and the young sisters be as the old sisters."

He knew at once he might as well have said them in German for all the good they did her. She was surprised when he pulled her against him and kissed her not very gently on the mouth. And he was surprised.

Her hands rested on his chest, against his wet shirt. Through the cloth came the warmth of his body along with the steady beating of his heart.

How his heart thumped against her palms! It hit so hard she believed, rather dizzy and breathless from the falling rain, that she had only to open his clothes in order to trace its shape and to behold its pulsing.

She began to undo his shirt, fumbling with the hooks and eyes. Underneath she found another layer: Menno's long underwear. Sticking her fingers through a gap in the placket, she touched the skin of his right breast and the hairs growing there.

She was confounded when Menno drew back: retreating, he who had always pursued.

This amused her so much that she laughed out loud. "Ah, Menno!" she said. "How shy you've grown!"

The rain was stopping. A few more drops fell and then there was only the dripping from the trees. He stood still, astounded. He had never heard her laugh. Nor had she ever called him "Menno."

— 7 —

Logan was thirsty. These days his mouth was continually dry. But Captina water didn't satisfy him.

"It's bitter," he told Dorsey. "It smells of chemi-
cals."

What he longed for was well water. The well water
they'd had at the farm. They had cranked it up on a long rope
from far below ground. The pail, speckled blue and white, sat
on a shelf. His grandmother or one of his aunts would hand
him down a dipperful. How sweet and cold it tasted!

"Cold and sweet," he said to Ursula. He said this as if
he were singing a song.

When his daughter was in the house, Logan was keenly
conscious of her every motion. She was like a floater in his
eye, a speck that moved here, moved there and wouldn't be
still; one that was forever sliding out of sight.

When she walked past, he felt the air stirred by her
body brush his face and it cheered him. Sometimes he reached
out and caught the hem of her dress and let it run through
his fingers. When he said, "Ursula," to her, her answer, "Yes,
Papa," came back warm and bright. She left him less often
now and he was glad.

She was an athletic, well-muscled girl. With her strong,
broad hands, her square-tipped fingers, she dexterously did
tasks he could no longer manage. She buttoned his shirt and
zippered his pants. Turned him on his bed. Pulled him up out
of chairs.

He was often awake in the night, and she read to him.
Her voice was soothing. She read until he fell asleep or until
the sun rose.

*

One morning in the hour before dawn, Papa asked her
to play the Victrola.

"You wrecked it. Don't you remember?" Dorsey told him, thinking he meant Mama's record-player. In fact, he'd knocked it to pieces with his fists. It was the morning after this event that Iva left.

But it was the gramophone on the farm he meant. The one that played blue-tinted records shaped like hollow soup cans. He wanted to hear the songs he'd listened to when he was eight or nine: minstrel tunes and ragtime piano.

Afterwards, when he asked for these old recordings, she switched on the radio instead and sometimes that was all right but other times it wasn't. Once when the radio played rock and roll, he'd thrown his chamber pot at it.

All that winter it seemed to Dorsey she beheld her papa's past risen about him in knee-high stacks, like brittle sheets of old newspapers. The house seemed full of their rustling.

Afternoons, as therapy, Dorsey tipped buttons from the button box out across the table or threw down a handful of pennies. Sometimes Papa was cheerful picking them up. But sometimes he was cross and wouldn't touch them and so, she had to gather them back herself.

Sometimes she could coax him into covering a sheet of notepaper with circles and slanted lines. Sometimes he tore the paper into pieces.

He often refused to hold the broom handle through his crooked arms and across his back or to let her rub a smile into his face, or to talk into the mirror while they watched his moving lips.

"Don't push him" his doctors told Dorsey. "Keep him calm," they said. "Keep him happy."

Dorsey thought, *There has always been someone keeping Papa happy. It is a heavy job. It wore my mama out.* However, she believed she was better at it than her mother had been.

He ate very little. She fed him in small spoonfuls. Every day she boiled mush and puddings for him. He ate slowly. Often, like a teething child, saliva ran from the corners of his slightly open mouth. She wiped it away with the linen handkerchief on which one of his aunts had embroidered the letter 'L'. He watched everything she did with fixed, unblinking eyes. More and more his face was set and blank. And more and more he did strange things.

One day she found him at his desk and her heart leaped up since she supposed that, after a long spell of inactivity, he was working. But at once she saw that, instead of writing, he was moving the objects on the desktop. He did this with the studied precision of a chess player. He slid a pencil jar to the far-right corner, an eraser to the center, a paperweight (a lump of amber with a gnat in it) to the left corner.

"What are you doing, Papa?"

"They insist that I arrange my things," he said. "They want them to be just so."

"Who insists?" she asked him. But he didn't answer.

She watched him slowly drag the paste pot toward him and set it, balanced nicely, on the edge above his lap.

"Where has Toby got to?" was what he wanted to know.

"He went out last evening after supper and hasn't come back. I think he has a lady-friend down on some Amish farm." Papa sat suddenly full of gloom. "My back is cold," he told her with the querulous tone of one habitually misused.

That night Dorsey dreamed White Toby came and crouched on her chest and sucked her breath so that she woke gasping. A week later he was still missing. Papa didn't mention his absence again except once when he said, "He'll find his meals harder to come by if he's gone wild."

In the evenings after supper, they played word games or planned their next day's meals. Or they discussed needful work about the house and in the yard and garden, how this chore should be done and when that job had best be finished. *But regardless of their actual conversation,* Dorsey thought, *What he is saying to me is, "Good-bye." And what I am saying to him is, "Stay."*

And, for a while, he did stay. Not only stayed but improved. He began to bathe himself and to walk about inside the house, holding to the furniture. He even wrote a little each day, covering, perhaps, a quarter of a page with his pinched script.

*

Logan rose early each morning now. He insisted on wearing a clean shirt and a tie. He did it for *them*. To honor them: the authors.

Because, lately, they were always in the room with him. They hung in the air, slightly higher than his head so that, by tilting his chin, he could meet their eyes.

To the right were George Eliot, Walter Scott, Meredith, Dickens, and Fielding, to the left, Thackery, Thomas Hardy, and Lawrence. His authors. His household gods. His phantom lovers. He had read them as a boy. As a man, he had written their lives. Now here they were, watching over him. Reserved but attentive. Solemn and portentous.

His publishers wanted him to write about modern authors, but he always declined since they were strangers. These in his room were old acquaintances. Besides, these were the ones that had got it right: the sheep in the fold, the farm houses and the barns, the villages, the meadows and the forests, the tinkers and parsons and milkmaids.

Lawrence particularly got it right. Like Logan, he was a miner's son. And, like Logan, he'd had a mother who dominated and pampered him. In *Sons and Lovers,* he'd got it right.

The authors peered down, observing him. Now and then they spoke to one another, repeating their own beautiful, everlasting prose. Listening to them, although his face remained frozen, inside himself, Logan smiled.

— 8 —

One spring evening when Dorsey stepped out onto the back porch, she found Menno Yoder in the yard.

He stood like the Colossus of Rhodes, his feet planted wide apart, his body dark against the sinking sun.

Papa leaned in the doorway behind her looking out while Menno stood before her looking in so that she felt, for a moment, the dizzying sense of beholding a doppelganger. Then Papa turned back into the house, and Menno knelt and tightened the laces of his left boot.

Menno scarcely knew why he'd come. The World, Logan Bendler, stared out at him first from the doorway, now from a window. The door of the World's house stood open. Menno could look in and see the work of his own hands fastened to the unclean walls. This frightened him somewhat.

Dorsey said, "Have you come to take me roller skating?"

He understood, by this time, when she meant to tease him. Still, he answered her solemnly, "Live for pleasure, end in slavery," although he also knew she came up against each of his sayings violently as if she'd run full tilt into a wall.

Sitting down on the porch's edge, Dorsey talked to him about her father. She told Menno how she'd come across her father's unfinished life of the British writer, D. H. Lawrence, put away in a drawer. "It was," she said, "as if he'd wanted it out of his sight because it fretted him in some way." So, she had begun to work on it by herself. Following an outline he'd made years ago, she was blocking out chapters, collecting data from reference books. And she had been reading Lawrence's letters.

Seating himself beside her, Menno, taking his turn in the conversation, told her how, this day, he had cultivated the young corn. How he had taken a horse to be shod. Tomorrow he would attend an auction and buy dress goods for his mother and, for himself, an awl.

They had got into the habit, when they were together, of recounting to one another things they'd done while they were apart. Their ordinary doings exhausted, they touched on their secret musings.

"Mama," she began, while he, in his turn, responded, "Shem," and so they told over, each to the other, old sorrows with a mournful whispering.

They sat silent a while. Then as Menno began to enumerate the ways in which his sisters were occupying their time, Dorsey thought, *I would like to live that way. To live,* she thought, *honored and protected. Serving husband and family and community. Knowing needful work was expected of me, knowing myself capable of doing it well.*

How good it would be to belong to a dutiful sisterhood knit by the bonds of common tasks. There would be joy in scrubbing wood floors with silver sand, scouring tin-ware, baking loaves, husking corn, raking the house-yard. In wearing a brown dress, a black kerchief round her shoulders. There would be pleasure in hiding her bound hair under a white cap so that only her husband should know how it looked hanging loose, contentment in following old, well-worn ways, guided by the rhythm of the seasons and by the feeling, which Menno had described, of being in touch with the Everlasting. If indeed such a thing existed.

"And has Addie had her baby?" she asked him. "Are you an uncle?"

Of a sudden his face fell so markedly that she thought, alarmed, *She has died in childbirth.* But he told her, "Addie had a boy."

Later on, he spoke of the child again, saying, "He will be a dwarf."

Dorsey knew this was not unusual, that there were many dwarves among the People. Still she saw he was suffering and reached for him. His hand was so large hers disappeared into it. In leaning toward him she scratched her arm on a thorn where an old rose briar hung over the porch rail. The torn skin bled down onto her skirt, making a stain with the look of menstrual blood so that she blushed and laughed, and he laughed and of a sudden Menno's heart leaped up and he thought, *Living with her would be like living with a bird. Her laughter, which is like bird song, would never stop. Nor would the soaring.*

It was because of the blood on her skirt that Dorsey found Toby.

After Menno went home, she knelt beside the watering can to wet the blood spots. Behind the can lay Toby's bones. Bits of sinew, a puff of white fur clung to them still. She guessed wild dogs had caught him before he could reach the safety of the house.

She gathered Toby up, his fur and his bones, and placed him on a bare spot of earth, covering him with sticks and straw and last year's withered tomato vines. She added crumpled newspaper soaked with a little kerosene and lit the pyre, watching it blaze up furiously, orange and yellow, in the newly fallen night.

When the flames died down, Dorsey saw that Toby had been transmuted into something other than a cat, and she thought the ashes which had been his bones marked a spot where time and Menno's Everlasting had, for the shortest of moments, met.

She said nothing about Toby to her papa. She never knew from one day to the next quite what effect misfortune would have on him and so she kept, determinedly, to cheerful news.

— 9 —

On his best days Logan was able to believe his doctors mistaken in their diagnosis. He dared hope he would, after all, regain his health and enjoy a long, vigorous and productive old age.

Although he was now, for the most part, confined to a wheelchair, he found that, paradoxically, in certain important ways, he was free. For example, he was delivered from his agonizing shuffle and from his fear of falling.

The chair operated on a battery so that he could send it quickly along with a touch of his hand. Could back it up, wheel it around, dart here and there.

Ursula cleared paths for the wheelchair by moving the furniture against the walls or by removing it entirely.

Traveling about in the chair gave Logan a sense of vigor and power. It made him feel magnanimous. He sent Ursula out more often with her friends.

He ordered a large wooden loom from the pages of a crafts catalogue. The day it arrived at their door, Logan watched his daughter's face, infinitely pleased with himself, tickled that he could still surprise her.

The doctor had advised Logan to take a little wine each day. The alcohol made him talkative. Often, as he sipped from his glass, he told Dorsey stories, tales of his boyhood on the farm. He liked best to tell the tale of his first experience churning butter.

He described himself hilariously astride the old barrel-shaped churn, singing hymns at the top of his voice as he thumped the wooden dasher up and down between his bare, knobby little boy's knees. How his muscles ached, he said. How his head swam with the prolonged effort! "When the butter came," said Papa, "it was like winning a battle." He presented the butter to his family and watched them spread it on bread, then eat it hungrily. Thereafter he was a hero and a legend. His grandma and his sisters and his aunts never ceased to praise his churning.

Often, lifting his glass, Logan toasted Dorsey for her devotion, telling her, "I should have called you, 'Frieda.' Frieda stayed with Lawrence to the end," he said. "His thoughts were her jewels. His books were her children. That's the sort of wife I should have had."

This was as close as Papa had come to mentioning Iva in many years so that of a sudden Dorsey grew vaguely alarmed, suspecting there had been, perhaps, some ominous change in his condition.

Casting about for a way to get his mind off Frieda Lawrence, Dorsey decided she would weave a hanging for his bedroom wall. He could watch it take form. It would be a present for his sixty-first birthday.

She set about making drawings of the scene she meant to weave. It was to represent Great Grandma Bendler's kitchen. Here stood the pump beside the iron stove. There sat the honey-pot on the oilcloth-covered table. A basket of ear corn rested in one corner ready for the pigs, the chickens and the cows. And of course, in the other corner, the famous churn!

After she had drawn the kitchen to her liking, Dorsey planned the colors she would use: blue for the walls, white for the table-cover, the honey-pot: yellow and black, the stove, green.

She was able to find wool yarn in all these colors except the shade of green for the stove which was meant to suggest painted iron and which she could not come across in any store.

One afternoon, the elderly lady who had taught Dorsey to hook rugs came to the door carrying a present: a skein of dark green yarn with a metallic glint.

Dorsey was overjoyed. As she and Papa drank tea at this hour, she offered a cup to the rug-lady. Although she'd been feeling poorly and hadn't meant to stay, the lady accepted. They sat a while sipping and chatting until Logan's hand began to shake, spilling tea into his saucer. After that the lady left rather quickly. She was, however, in the kitchen long enough to fill it, unbeknownst to Dorsey or her father, with influenza virus.

Meanwhile as the days grew warmer, Dorsey reflected it would soon be time to plant the garden. Papa poured over seed catalogues. He wanted not only vegetables but herbs. Not only herbs but flowers. By summer he wished to see, in their garden space, all the blossoms that had grown at the home farm. "Columbine," said Papa. "Ragged robin, hollyhocks, calendula, foxglove, delphiniums and Canterbury bells." As to herbs, he selected sage, mint, thyme, fennel, rosemary and basil.

One night he grew so excited over these garden plans that his tremors markedly increased. Dorsey had to dim the lights and massage him with coconut oil before he could fall asleep.

As she covered him, Dorsey saw his slender, restless feet moving continually in his sleep as if he were walking to many places, he who, awake, could walk nowhere.

Does Mama still walk about somewhere in the world? Dorsey wondered. For always in her mind's eye she saw Iva going a journey that never ended, that was always happening.

Dorsey had lately fallen into the habit of weaving people and places in her mind. Now, sitting by her father's bedside, listening to his breathing, she began to weave her mother. Drowsily, half-laughing at what she did, she wove in her thoughts a woman of gold and silver threads and copper wires. A red-headed woman, stylized like a figure in a Navajo rug. Her dress was the color of a cloudy opal.

"When I shook, they shimmered. When I shimmied, they shook," Mama said in Dorsey's mind, describing, as she'd used to do, the dresses she'd worn back in her days as a vocalist. "To be the one dress among the jackets and bowties," Mama said. "To be the canary. And, after each song, to hear the applause!"

'Marie, the dawn is breaking,' Mama had sung. *'I get no kick,'* Mama explained. *'I'll never smile again',* even on *'the sunny side of the street,'* because *'you ain't got a thing if you ain't got that swing.'*

Papa coughed and muttered. Dorsey, leaning over his bed, grabbed his shoulders and turned him onto his side.

— 10 —

The next morning Dorsey filled out the seed order. When the time came for preparing the ground, however, she made little headway, the pressure of her foot being too light to sink the spade properly into the tightly clenched soil. Eventually a summons for aid went out from the house on the edge of Captina to the fields below. The one who responded was Menno Yoder.

The afternoon he appeared at the door, the weather was

warm enough for Logan to sit outside in his wheelchair and watch the work go forward. Menno, with ease, drove in the spade to its upper rim and lifting it, filled with earth, flipped it over. The turned soil, a deep brown color and rich-looking as hair, shone in the sun, warming and drying.

Dorsey chopped up the clods with a hoe, then raked them fine as corn meal using a vigorous back and forth motion. Though a cold wind now and again swept the garden, no cloud crossed the sun. Dorsey and Menno, commencing to sweat from their labors, shed their wraps. As they worked, they talked in subdued voices, laughing when, haply, their tools clanged together or if they accidentally showered one another with dirt. But always they were reminded by Logan's fierce gaze that this hour was not about conviviality but about gardening, a serious business.

When Logan fell asleep, they wheeled him into the house and lifted him onto his bed. Afterward they talked more freely.

Dorsey told Menno of the wall-hanging she was working in wool yarn. Menno told Dorsey of the 'grandpa house' he and his father and brothers were building, joined to the main farmhouse by a breezeway. When it was finished, Menno said, his grandparents would move into it and Menno's father would take the burden of farming off the older man's shoulders.

"The grandparents will have tasks to do," Menno explained, "but lighter ones. And we can care for them as it grows needful. Just as," he added, "you now care for your father."

Dorsey looked toward the house. "When your grandparents are gone," she said, "you'll still have your parents, your brothers and sisters, your aunts and uncles, and all your cousins." She paused. "Even if all of these were taken, you would still have the People. When Papa's gone, I'll have no one."

You'll have me, Menno wanted to say but he held the words back and instead mentioned a thing he'd been wanting to tell her. "If you turned Amish," he said, "you would have the People, too."

Dorsey stopped her raking.

"If you joined us," he explained. "If you took up our ways, lived as we live. If you believed as we believe."

Dorsey closed her eyes, imagining this.

Menno was encouraged since she didn't at once say 'no.' However, neither did she say 'yes.'

After a time, what Dorsey did say was "Do you remember the night we danced in the barn? It happened that, when I walked to the house, I met your grandfather coming down the front steps, and he and I looked up at the moon together. I said to him, "To think men have walked there!" He said to me, "This never happened."

Menno shrugged and laughed. "He thinks it's just a wild tale. A lie the Worlds tell. What does it matter?"

But she fixed him with her intense, dark eyes, saying, "How can it not matter?" And to this he found no ready reply.

Sometimes when they were together, they talked of the future and now Dorsey began speaking of how, when her papa was dead, she would take his ashes, as she had promised him, to the Kiowa Ranch in New Mexico and sprinkle them on D. H. Lawrence's grave. She would ride a train or a bus or an airplane. Then she would come back and finish his book.

Menno talked of traveling, too, since the men of his sect often went on journeys before they married and settled down. One man went south and, ever afterward, was called, "Alabama." Many had gone to Pennsylvania to visit the Amish there. Sometimes they brought back wives.

Menno spoke of his desire to see the West.

Afterward, Dorsey suffered pangs of guilt and of superstitious fear. She thought, *I said, "when Papa is dead." Will this cause him to die soon?* And she lived a day or two trembling and a-prey to spells of hidden weeping.

And Menno likewise suffered guilt and fear because he admitted to himself, *If I went west with her, I would never again leave her and I would be lost like Shem.*

Menno walked home glancing back over his shoulder at a bright star which seemed balanced on the roof of the house in which the World, Logan Bendler, was dying. In which Dorsey, defying God, fought to preserve his life. A night breeze moved in the pines, sighing with a human voice. Menno shivered, grown, of a sudden, afraid for Dorsey's soul.

He knew people exchanged their souls for unaccountable things. Shem had bartered his for an automobile. Dorsey would sell hers for her papa, to keep him alive. There was no question in Menno's mind that she would. And if Menno knew this, the Devil knew it also.

In his secret heart, Menno had always believed that Hell was not full of fire as some had it, but was made, instead, of ice. He pictured it as resembling the icehouse stacked to the ceiling with frigid blue-white blocks. Or like the lake when the men had finished cutting the blocks: a part still covered by thick life-withering ice and a bared part presenting an expanse of black water too dead to give back a reflection.

When he thought of Shem in such a place, Menno wept.

His elder brother had, in fact, spoken of Hell that last night in the barn. "It's not underground nor in the future, Menno," Shem had said. "It's here. It's now."

But how was Menno to come at an understanding of this, how ask Shem for an explanation since the Bishop had decreed his brother must be shunned. While he hesitated, it became too late. Their father arrived and drew Menno away from Shem and into the house.

Shem had been a harness-maker. He had loved the scent of leather, the supple feel of it under his fingers. Menno knew that as a boy he'd loved the work of the farm: bundling oats, binding fodder and raking hay, together with his brothers.

He'd loved going to worship service every other Tuesday. And corn huskings. And sings.

Growing older, he had strained against the old ways. He had turned his eyes ahead toward the sinful, shifting world instead of back toward the sacred unchanging martyrs.

Menno went now into that same barn where Shem had hung lifeless from a harness strap and sat on the floor in his usual spot near the horses. Sitting there he sang to himself the hymn, "Awake, a voice is calling us." He sang, *"Wacht Auf ruft uns die Stimme."*

And after he had sung, he rested his thoughts on the holy books, each in turn. On the *Ausband*, the hymnal, on the *Ordnung*, the body of rules, and on the *Martyrs' Mirror*. When he named them aloud, these titles seemed to form themselves into presences like pillars of fog or smoke that stood before him to lead and comfort him.

Because the truth was that he sometimes feared, not only for Dorsey's soul, but for his own. Often he had sinful thoughts. Evil feelings. He hated the Bishop for the shunning, hated his father for pulling him away from Shem that fateful night. It now occurred to him that these feelings together with his attraction to Dorsey had perhaps been the reason for his sister, Addie, birthing a dwarf child. Because the God of the Amish was a jealous god. A vengeful one.

Certainly Menno knew that, regardless of the cause, a family must accept what God sends to it. *But suppose,* Menno thought, *such a birth isn't just punishment for sin but has a deeper, more terrible significance? Suppose it is a revelation of the nature of the divine itself.* The hairs on Menno's nape stood as he saw, Devil-sent, the figure of God rising before his mind's eye, small and twisted: a dwarf with the Bishop's face.

— 11 —

That night Dorsey lay on her bed thinking, as she often did, of the seedling trees she and Menno had planted.

It seemed to her she could feel them growing far off on the hillside and down in the dim woods. Feel their roots reaching for water, spreading thirstily into the welcoming earth, and feel, too, the doe moving through the bushes, brushing against them.

All through the night, these intuitions came and went strangely in her brain like an intermittent vertigo.

She spent the next morning working on the tapestry of Great Grandma Bendler's kitchen. After she had laid out the warp threads on the loom and attached the ends on the horizontal beams, she used the foot pedal to start up the heddle and began to pass the shuttle through the shed, pushing each row close to the one before with the comb-like reed. She worked most of the day while Papa watched from his wheelchair.

Two days later when Logan began to run a temperature, they supposed he had caught cold sitting in the windy garden. When his illness worsened, father and daughter knew it for the influenza that was breaking out everywhere in Captina, an influenza impervious to preventative shots.

Logan kept to his bed and dutifully swallowed down medicines with his buttermilk. After four days he began a deep, shattering cough.

Now and again Papa shook with chills. He complained of pain in his chest. His fever rose. One day he brought up blood in his sputum. Pneumonia, the doctors told Dorsey, and began to talk of moving him to a hospital.

But Papa wanted to stay at home, and so they went on a while as they were. Papa had honey for his cough and penicillin shots. He had his head raised on pillows to improve his breathing.

Sometimes his mind was extremely clear. At other times he seemed to be writing books. Now and again, he talked rather wildly of buying a cow.

Each day when Dorsey bathed and dressed her father's bent and shrunken body, she saw the framework of his bones plainer and plainer under his skin. She trembled, tracing the patterns they made, and her knees weakened.

Soon she lost her sense of the hour, the day, the week, even of this place where they were together. She gripped Papa close with her hands and her mind held him. Every night she fell asleep exhausted by the effort, and every morning she took it up, the act, the feat of holding on. Sometimes she felt that he was sucking life out of her body into his, and she was glad.

In her effort to keep him alive, Dorsey found herself focusing on him more and more tightly until, in her memories, only he stood firm: Logan of the stubborn spirit and haunted eyes. Her beautiful papa roamed her every thought with his graceful rolling walk and his roguish grin.

On the day before they took him to the hospital, Logan raised himself in his bed and told Dorsey, "Bugs are running on the walls!"

Dorsey saw no bugs. Yet he saw them. He was, in fact, beside himself with fear of them. "Kill them!" he begged her. "Kill them!" He shrieked the words until they rent her eardrums.

So she took off her shoe and hit the rubber heel up and down the walls making black marks on the paper.

The next morning when they laid him on a stretcher to carry him to the ambulance, he appeared to see nothing. His body, his limbs, his neck and head seemed made of metal rusted into immobility.

*

Incredibly, in the hospital room, this new, clean place, the same loathsome insects crept up and down the walls. Logan fixed them with an unblinking stare. He feared to close his eyes lest they began to drop onto him and devour his flesh. As always there were women around him. These wore white dresses. They fussed and twiddled, trying to do him good. The bugs, however, went on crawling up and down the walls.

Toward evening, Logan felt in himself, in his body, a heavy sinking. It was as if the mattress were made of some viscous material in which he was becoming increasingly embedded.

For a time, he napped. When he woke, he had no idea where he was.

Dorsey sat beside her father watching, above his head, the electrical patterns made by the beating of his heart. He lay in a tangle of cables and switches, of tubes and wires and bottles. She wished to embrace him but could find no part of his body left free.

"Papa," she said.

Although his eyes were open, he didn't shift his gaze from the opposite wall.

In place of hugging him, she held his left foot. Slender and warm beneath her fingers, it seemed full of life. However, his skin had taken on a bluish tinge and his sputum, the color of prune juice, was viscid and stringy. He breathed with a halting, strangled rasp as if he were drowning.

Just before 11 P.M., sitting upright on her chair, still holding to Papa's foot, Dorsey fell into a doze. Struggling to come awake, she had the odd, fleeting sensation of being a candle inside a skull. She felt herself flickering. Flickering, she shone out the eyeholes, the nose-hole, the ear-holes, the mouth. Then, instead of the skull, it was the mirror ball that held her. Swinging above the skaters where the wind of their going buffeted her, she broke into a brightness that showered out over the room and became one with the pattern the skaters made as they circled.

Coming fully awake, Dorsey found the hiss of the skaters' wheels had become the sound of the oxygen feeding into Papa's lungs. His eyes were closed now. He seemed to be resting more peacefully.

Around 3 A.M. there began to be gaps in Logan's breathing. He raised his hands and, curling his fingers, held them, one above the other, as he moved them together up, then down, up, then down.

"He's searching for something," the night nurse said.

"He's shooing something away," said the nurse's aide.

But Dorsey, considering the matter several days after Logan's death, thought that she alone knew what he'd been doing. He'd been churning.

*

Logan's funeral was held at the local mortuary. His publisher came. Also a few of Dorsey's Captina friends, together with certain tradesmen and passing acquaintances. The rug-lady, recovered now from her flu, brought a basket of anemones.

Menno Yoder sat uneasily on a chair by the door. He wore his white shirt with a faint sense of betrayal since his mother had sewed it to be his covering at Tuesday worship.

He had supposed the World's funeral would resemble a worship service, but this was not so. No hymns were sung. No sermon was preached, no scripture given. Instead, those attending listened solemnly to passages read out from unclean sources which were to Menno, incomprehensible.

Afterward, the World's body, at his own request, was reduced to ash and placed in a small tin box. Menno stood beside Dorsey as she received this box. When they walked out of the crematorium, it became necessary for him to steady her by gripping her left elbow with his right hand.

Dorsey carried the metal box home and placed it on the table beside her bed. What she thought was this: *For one who had, his life-long, so stubbornly resisted change, Papa had become, in spite of himself, very changed indeed.*

— 12 —

Though she tried hard, Dorsey could not recover from the shock of her father's death. Neither her mind nor her body seemed able to heal.

Her thoughts bent in her brain as if passing through a prism which spread them bewilderingly giving them many an odd color.

Each day she expected to find Papa at his desk, lying on his bed or sitting in the garden. And each day he was none of these places.

She listened for his voice to say, "Ursula." For the sound of his chair, the whine of its motor, the turning of its wheels. Or for his coughing in the night.

Whenever she glimpsed, from her eye-corner, a rolled-up blanket or a shadowed cushion, she thought with relief, *There he is!* and felt, for the briefest of moments, in company with him again.

In Dorsey's body, the denial of Logan's death took the form of dizzying, thunderous vibrations deep inside the canals of her ears and of a neuralgia that worried the bones of her face.

After a time, the ache moved from her face to her shoulders and thighs, then out into her limbs where it became like a cracking open of her long bones so that the marrow seemed to lay exposed and crumbling.

When people came to the door, Dorsey turned them away. Even the rug-lady. Even Addie, Menno's sister. Even Menno himself.

She ate and slept very little. She spent most of each day walking about the house touching things Papa had touched. However, his hands had left behind no marks and no warmth. Even the books he'd written stood, slick and cold in their embossed jackets, unyielding as slabs of ice.

*

One day Dorsey sat down at the loom and began to undo her weaving. She had worked a section of the blue wall and nearly all of the green stove. She used scissors and a knitting needle to pick loose the yarn, pulling it from the loom with her fingers, piling the scraps and pieces on the floor at her feet. It was the first action she'd taken since Papa's death that gave her satisfaction. That let her feel, briefly, a sort of peace.

When the loom stood naked against her bedroom wall, she let her hands drop to her sides. She wished to do no more weaving. She found herself hankering after a truth beyond patterns of her own making, if it were only the reality of the empty loom.

Besides, the reason for the weaving was gone. Papa would have no more birthdays.

Every day, the house was empty. The garden was empty. The village and the world were empty. Ursula could find no function for herself in such emptiness.

"My life is dross," she said aloud into the empty house. Hearing her own voice say this word, 'dross,' she wondered how it had got onto her tongue.

Almost at once she knew it for Papa's word.

"You don't know what those days on the farm meant to me!" Papa had told her more than once. "All life since has been dross."

So that Dorsey had understood from an early age that Mama was dross and she, herself, was also dross, and she'd felt herself drop into darkness.

Now she wondered what their time together, hers and Papa's, would have been if he had loved her more than he loved his childhood memories. Or, if he had loved Mama more, what their days as husband and wife could have amounted to.

As time passed and passed again, Dorsey came to feel that she hung motionless in her life like a fish at the bottom of a frozen pond. Or like a figure in a tapestry. Then one day, the seeds came.

The postman banged on the door, and when she opened it, he thrust into her arms a large flat box wrapped in brown paper.

She carried it to the kitchen table and, taking up the shears, ripped open one end and dumped out the contents with such force that it spilled across the table and onto the seat of one of the chairs and from thence out over the linoleum floor.

There they lay in their bright-colored packets: all the seeds Papa had selected. Pictured on the covers were the plants he'd wanted to see, to smell, to touch this summer in the garden.

Dorsey sat on the floor and gathered the seeds into her lap. Smoothing the packets, she shook them to make them rattle. At first she was saddened by the seeds. She almost threw the packets into the trash. But then she thought, *I'll plant Papa's garden.* The next morning, for the first time in many days, Dorsey rose with a purpose. The tapestry had been her project; the garden had been Papa's. She saw it as one of the final gifts she could give him.

Raking the soil once again, she used the hoe handle to mark out rows. She knelt beside each row scattering seed, pinching the earth back together, patting it down with her palms.

The package contained a great many packets. Dorsey was nearly a week and a half planting them. She scattered certain of the flower seeds in circular beds and in square and rectangular patches. She bought a hose and a nozzle and watered the seeds with a fine spray.

As she worked at planting the garden, Dorsey's flesh warmed and her skin was bathed in sweat. At the same time, her thoughts and her feelings seemed to thaw and loosen in her and to resume their accustomed flowing. At first, however, they flowed only backward.

Dorsey recalled how, long ago on a certain day in Tapp City, she had watched Papa hit a golf ball. He drew back the club, stood a moment contemplating the ball, then made a mighty swing. The ball took to the air like a bird. She had tried to follow it, but it disappeared into the burning summer sky. After a time, it fell onto the far-off green like an egg laid by an eagle in flight.

Mama, who didn't play, often walked about the course with Papa looking for lost tees for his use. Dorsey washed Papa's golf balls in a machine like a churn. She moved the handle up and down and the balls were scrubbed by soapy brushes. She dried them on a striped towel.

"I'll teach you to play," Papa always said. But he never did. Most summers he entered golf competitions. Amateur contests sponsored by local businessmen. At last, he won. Happy and proud, he went often to look at the cup. No doubt it stood yet in its glass case at the golf club proclaiming Logan Bendler champion of the Westside Merchant's 1962 Amateur Golf Tournament. Even when Papa was no more, the cup would still be there.

"What lasts forever?"

Dorsey had asked her father that question only a week before he died, prompted, most likely, by Menno's claims concerning the eternal Amish. Papa hadn't hesitated.

"Some novels," he'd said. "But not all novels."

Now, thinking of this conversation, Dorsey decided that, since Papa had gone on to say that certain of Lawrence's novels were everlasting, he was justified in wishing his ashes scattered on Lawrence's grave. Clearly, it was his way of joining himself to the eternal: he who could not write eternal books but could only read them.

The next day Dorsey began to make preparations to fulfill her promise to carry her father's ashes to New Mexico.

— 13 —

Menno Yoder, for all his admiration of the West, tried to talk her out of going. "What good will it do?" he asked her. And he said, "It was a foolish promise." Because no one doubted that the World's mind had been clouded by his illness. The object of the trip struck Menno as idiotic.

"After I've scattered Papa's ashes," Dorsey told him, "I'll come home and finish his Lawrence biography."

"And then what will you do?"

But no answer came to her.

They were seated on a bench in the garden. It had rained during the night. The wet soil smelled strongly sweet and warm and she thought of the seeds stirring in it. And of the plowing and planting Menno had come from, in the land below Captina.

She thought, *How calm he is, how confident in his Amishness. Sitting in the sun, resting from his labor, he is like a rock, or like a tree, growing.*

And she wished, not for the first time, to be as Menno was: serene. Well-ordered and content.

"'Be not conformed to this world,'" Menno quoted, since he feared she would lose herself in the vastness and the evil of the country and, after all, not come back.

Perhaps, Dorsey thought, *it's a good thing to go about with your head full of your forefathers' sayings. It's certainly too painful,* she told herself, *and too difficult to make up your own.*

"I'd always supposed," she reminded him, "we'd make this trip west together."

He had supposed this, too. But the timing was very bad. The plowing and the planting wouldn't wait. His hands were sorely needed by his family. And by all the People.

"I'll ride the bus with you," he offered, "to North Darlington. To the train station. I'll see you off on the train."

What she thought was this: *Maybe he'll ride the train as well.* And her spirits lifted. She had a feeling of the future scrolling out in front of her like a finely woven linen sheet. However, Menno drove off in his bachelor buggy leaving the matter of the train trip unresolved.

She had always known, of course, how Menno regarded her promise to her father: this scattering of his ashes, Menno who had never read Lawrence. Nor Hardy. Nor Scott, nor Meredith. If he knew of their novels at all, no doubt he thought of them as worldly and sinful. Like moonwalking.

Since there was no way of justifying her travel plans to him, Dorsey thought this: *When the time comes to go, I'll go. What Menno does then will be up to him.*

*

Dorsey found the satchel Papa had used for carrying his golf shoes, shirt and knickers. It was fitted with a shoulder strap and was large enough to hold the amount of clothing and food she intended to take.

She packed carefully, placing the metal box containing Logan's ashes in a protected place between two blouses and positioning the food in easy reach at the top.

The day she walked into the bus station, Menno was there waiting for her.

As he waited, Menno had thought that, now the World, Logan, was dead, it was possible Dorsey would agree to marry him. That she would join the People and take up his beliefs. As Ruth in the Bible had transferred her caring and her loyalty from her husband to her mother-in-law, so might Dorsey change hers from Logan to him.

A certain uneasiness had touched Menno as he considered these projections. *For,* he told himself, *if this Outsider girl becomes Amish like the young sisters and the old sisters, then what pulled me to her may be lost.* And he speculated that he might then find her without spark or savor as he now found Naomi.

On the other hand, Dorsey might marry him but refuse to join the Amish. Always, she was unpredictable. And of course, it was possible she would ride away on the train and never come back. In which case, the only safe thing to do was to board the train with her. Because, for all his speculation, of a sudden he felt he could not bear a life without her.

*

From his seat on the bus, Menno watched the fields, the houses, the roads, the silos and barns fly by. He had often made this trip to North Darlington. All the sights were familiar. Yet they were also strange because this time she was beside him. And because of what might happen when the ride was over.

They had settled on the left hand side of the bus so that when the driver turned toward North Darlington, the afternoon sun came through the windows and licked Menno's head, then spilled into his lap. Just such a bright warmth had touched him like a blessing as he sat, earlier that week, astride a roof-beam helping the other men build a barn.

Far below he'd heard a mallet strike on a chisel head with a steady, chonking rhythm and, looking down, he'd seen one of the deacons hollowing out a mortise joint from a slab of timber. He'd watched a curl of red oak as the chisel skinned it off. Flecks of oak and sawdust lay scattered over the deacon's barndoor pants.

What Menno thought was this: *If I go on the train with Dorsey, I may, in the end, lose this fellowship. Lose barn-raising and preaching, plowing and planting, huskings and sings.* And now he asked himself, *If need be, could I give them up?*

He answered that he could. But even as he answered, cold like a killing frost settled over him and he shivered in the sunshine.

What communion hath light and darkness? It was one of the elders' voices speaking in his head. *Since her father's passing, this Outsider girl's eyes had been like black wells. Perhaps her soul, too, was dark. And yet she had also about her such a surpassing brightness. Her hair glinted in the sun and her fair skin flickered.*

Thinking this, Menno's heart thumped in his chest and, of a sudden, for the first time, he knew he would forfeit his own soul without hesitation in order to be with Ursula Bendler.

When they reached North Darlington where Dorsey boarded the train, Menno boarded with her.

— 14 —

Once they'd climbed aboard, Dorsey wanted to ride the train forever. Wanted to travel on and on without purpose or destination and never arrive at journey's end.

However, from the bag at her feet, the funerary box pushed so hard upon her consciousness that, like it or not, she was again consumed by the mission of its delivery.

They ate peanuts, stuffing the shells into their pockets, and apples and pears. Menno juggled three pears until one escaped him and rolled under the seat of a sleeping passenger across the aisle. Whereupon, they got the giggles, both Dorsey and Menno, and hid their faces against each other's shoulders and felt, the two of them, very foolish. And very young.

They napped with their coats wrapped about their knees, Dorsey's head in Menno's lap. When they neared Chicago, they peeled oranges and fed the sections to one another, mopping their faces with Menno's red bandanna handkerchief when the juice spurted from their mouth corners.

At Chicago they switched trains. The new train sped away quickly into darkness. Looking out the window, Menno and Dorsey saw their own faces looking back. Menno was amazed to behold himself heading west.

Riding the train, Dorsey began to visualize, in the far distance, a blue-green frothing against dark rocks: the Pacific Ocean.

As a child she had pored over pictures in Mama's *Geographics* of this great salt-water expanse. Now she felt its presence plainly, immense and heaving, along the western rim.

Before she slept, Dorsey dutifully thought of home. Of Papa's bed with, still on its mattress, the imprint of his body where it had lain so many hours. And of his empty chair.

Menno was already sleeping, his head against Dorsey's shoulder. His hat was pushed back and the moon, reaching through the window, touched his yellow hair.

Dorsey remembered how, the night before she set out for the bus station, the moon had been so bright it kept her awake. Finally, she'd gotten out of bed and walked about the house from living room to dining room to kitchen. She'd opened the kitchen door and as she stood looking out, she'd heard a cry. A high, thin wail somewhere out in the night.

At first, she took it for a yowling cat. She imagined Toby crying like that when the dogs were after him and no one to open the door. And she thought how she had burnt his bones and scattered dirt over the ashes.

But then she'd seen an owl silhouetted against the moon: a great dark presence sailing above the woodlot, gripping a small animal in its talons.

Beside her on the train, Menno straightened and, still asleep, resettled his hat so that the wide, flat brim shaded his face.

Dorsey wondered, *Does he wear his hat in bed?* And she wondered if she would learn the answer only if she were to marry him.

Dorsey began to feel more and more anxious about getting to Kiowa Ranch and scattering Logan's ashes since she understood she could in no way decide how to go on with her life until this deed was done.

*

Certain things in Chicago turned Menno uneasy. Also, certain things in Kansas. In Chicago, they went to the World Trade Center. From behind glass, Menno watched people who were not farmers monitoring, on charts, the sales of cattle, corn, oats and wheat. Not only in the present, but in the future.

Menno thought of the auctions the People held on Saturdays at home where live cattle bawled and pigs grunted and grain and vegetables lay in bushel baskets and where farmers and their wives walked about examining everything, buying and selling and visiting with their neighbors. By comparison, the World Trade Center seemed to Menno empty and dull. Yet it was full of the unseen presences and of black magic.

Walking back to the train station, Menno and Dorsey saw many shiny and beautiful automobiles, both parked along the curbs and moving up and down the streets, so that Menno thought, *This day the Devil is showing me the kingdoms of the earth. How many such sights had Shem seen as he was tempted before he fell from grace?*

*

Going through Kansas, Menno saw many head of cattle crushed together, shut up in vast feedlots. He saw towering grain elevators, and endless stretches of wheat and corn growing, and he knew his farm to be like a dot and the whole Knox County settlement of the People to be like a speck compared to these enormous fields. And again, he felt that he looked into the future and that the future was alien to him.

Sometimes he saw a farmer shut up in a cab of metal and glass, high atop a huge tractor. Menno watched him going his solitary way, turning a furrow that stretched to the setting sun. Seeing this, loneliness formed like a scum of ice on Menno's soul, and he was homesick for his brothers.

However, when the train reached New Mexico, Dorsey sat on his lap the better to see the passing scene, and as, pressing their heads together, they watched the mountains rise up along the horizon, he felt in company and content. At night in the darkened coach, they whispered together, their warm breath falling on one another's faces.

Through the long hours they grew giddy with the rocking of the train and with the moonlit land spinning past. Their journey began to feel like a Biblical wandering so that when Menno slid his tongue into Dorsey's mouth for the first time, it seemed to both of them a seal set on a covenant.

— 15 —

Now and again, they had adventures. Once, when the train made a brief stop, Dorsey climbed out onto the platform to find a number of Navajo women selling jewelry they had fashioned from turquoise and silver.

The women had spread necklaces and rings, bracelets and earrings on wooden tables. The tourists passed among the tables inspecting their wares.

Dorsey stepped toward them just as a man accidentally brushed against one of the tables, upsetting it, flinging slender, glittering pieces onto the platform.

Helping to gather up the spilt jewelry, Dorsey observed that the young women touched each piece comfortingly, as you would touch a bruised and weeping child.

Dorsey bought three necklaces. Back on the train, she admired their intricate patterns. They felt pliant and faintly warm as if heat from the fingers of the silversmith remained in the metal.

That afternoon while Dorsey napped, Menno took his way to the lounge car and sat staring out through the great windows. Hour on hour he watched the plains pass by. Thus far he had seen more than enough of the West to know it was not what he had expected it to be. He wasn't so much disappointed as he was disturbed, in some fundamental way, to his heart's core.

The land was gray. The grass was withered. Land and grass were both unutterably dry. He saw evidence, however, that, on occasion, there must have been too much water. The very soil had been washed away. There were barren gullies with, on their sides, scoured, exposed rock. Scarcely any dwellings or people or livestock were to be seen.

Shem had told him, "Hell is here. It is now," and indeed it seemed to Menno he beheld its landscape unrolling before his eyes. Nothing grew on the arid soil except for dark, stunted bushes, hunched dwarf-like on the far-off hills. Menno felt the desolation as a pain shooting through his eye sockets. *I could not live in such emptiness!* he thought.

He saw a coyote passing down a slope, starving and furtive and, in a burst of terror, felt that he discerned his own soul wandering aimless in a place without faith or meaning, purpose or duty, design or hope.

Beside him on the table stood a basket filled with small bottles of wine. He took one, uncorked it, and drank. And then drank another and another, trying to bring buoyancy back to his sinking spirits.

And he thought, just before the confusion of alcohol fogged his brain, *I am here because my blood burns for her, but think of the martyrs dropped from ladders into fire, who burned indeed and yet did not recant!*

He began to see himself as self-indulgent and weak of will and he was ashamed.

Being homesick, Menno commenced, during the journey, to speak to Dorsey of the farms he knew around Captina. He described the farmland they would buy there and the house they would build with the help of the People. He imagined for her the wedding they would have and the presents they would receive.

Dorsey, listening to his talk, fell easily into a daydream in which she saw spare, clean rooms, scoured floors and shining pots. In which she walked through many-colored, fragrant flowerbeds, and watched children, hers and Menno's, playing about the houseyard.

For, truth to tell, she was tired of traveling. Weary of the pressure of her mission. Often, she pictured Papa's ashes floating down like gray birds to settle on Lawrence's mound. She projected the deed done. The promise kept. And life going on. She began to admit that, in some hidden, basic way, she yearned to rest in Menno. To be "Right with God" as Menno was. As the Amish were. More and more it brought her a deep contentment to imagine herself spending her life "Strengthening the things which remain."

Only the Sangre de Christos troubled her contentment. She had never before looked on such high mountains. They startled her, these sharp, snowy peaks which seemed to stride over the land! They rose up, now here, now there, appearing to move about like giants. Or like great-shouldered gods who stared at her from one point, then from another.

"Blood of Christ," she whispered to herself. "Blood of Christ." And indeed, at sunset the summits turned the red of wounds. The very landscape reminded her of death. The thin flesh of the soil stretched over sharp bone-like rocks reminded her of Logan's body as it had been at the end.

And she thought, *Menno is right to resist change. For see how Papa went from living flesh to corpse to ash. Once a man, now he is nothing.* The word *nothing* echoed and re-echoed in her brain. All at once this trip seemed futile and she believed Menno had been right when he called her vow a foolish promise.

*

Sometimes Dorsey and Menno talked with fellow travelers, now from their seats, now in the lounge car. To certain people Dorsey tried to explain the promise she had made to her father. It was as if by sharing it she would validate its execution. No one with whom she spoke knew Lawrence's work except one young man who had studied it briefly in college and had come away with a low opinion of it.

"Most of his stuff is second rate," he told Dorsey. "Some of it is awful. At best, it's uneven. If I were you," the young man said, "I'd pick some other writer to sprinkle my dad on."

Dorsey and Menno got off the train at Albuquerque and rented a car. As they drove toward the Lawrence ranch near Taos, Dorsey reflected how, very soon now, Papa's wish would be fulfilled, and they would start back to Captina. The thought cheered her.

They followed a steep winding road through meadows where cattle grazed, red ones and black, all wild-looking. Some of them were belled.

High up among pines, a gravel road turned off and ended at the ranch.

When she climbed out of the car, Dorsey caught her breath. They had arrived at a gathering of mountains! It was as if, all this time, the peaks had been traveling across the plains on purpose to meet them at this place. She reached out her hand thinking, almost, to touch the snow on their summits, so close they seemed to have drawn in the clear, thin air.

When she pulled out the funerary box, Dorsey fancied the mountains looked disapproving. It was as if they wanted life and she instead had brought them death.

Now that the time was come to dispose of Papa's ashes, she was of a sudden filled with a foreboding that some mishap would prevent her doing the deed.

Dorsey and Menno toiled, together with the caretaker of the ranch and a number of tourists, up the slope toward Lawrence's grave.

Below them they saw a green valley with, around it, rings of low mountains: blue lines of ridges and, peering over them, ivory pinnacles so profoundly silent, so transcendent in size they seemed to stare down from another time and another place.

Dorsey carried the metal box under her arm. She had disguised it by wrapping it in Menno's bandanna handkerchief. She eyed the caretaker warily, thinking perhaps he might object to her plan once he knew of it. But she thought, *I'll lag behind and do it quickly so that no one sees.*

Stones had been used to make a path which mounted the hill at a sharp pitch. Each time she stopped to recover her breath, Dorsey looked toward the top but could see nothing. At last, she made out a roof on which the statuette of a bird appeared to perch.

In fact, on the hill's crest there stood a sort of garish mock-chapel of the size and general appearance of a child's playhouse. It had two tiny round windows and a narrow door. It was three-sided and somewhat shabby, the white paint peeling from its plaster walls.

Inside, two small, freshly cut pine trees had been placed on either side of a cement altar, some three feet high by four feet wide. Pinecones and brown-needled branches littered the floor. A walking-stick of twisted wood stood in one corner. A tall metal candlestick with the unlit stub of a candle in it leaned against the wall.

"But where is Lawrence?" Dorsey said rather forlornly to Menno as the others passed out of the chapel. Menno, who had listened closely to what the caretaker had to say, pointed to the altar.

"He's there," said Menno. "He's mixed in with the cement."

Dorsey stared at the block. Then pressing the box tight to her chest, she stepped out of the chapel, joining the tourists.

His wife, Freida, had done it, of course. So that Mabel Dodge and certain of the women who followed after Lawrence couldn't steal him away, ash though he was.

The caretaker laughed, telling the tale. And the tourists laughed, listening.

Dorsey, feeling cold to her marrow, fixed her eyes on the plaster phoenix, Lawrence's symbol of immortality. Its neck, she saw, was cracked through.

They went down the hill then and stood in a group while the caretaker pointed out the cabin where Lawrence and Freida had lived. It had in it, he said, a table, chairs and a row of shelves, all of which were built by Lawrence. It was, however, kept locked away from the public.

The caretaker ended by pointing out the great tree beside the cabin under which the artist, Georgia O'Keeffe, had painted her famous picture of stars shining down through its limbs and branches. "The everlasting stars," Dorsey whispered to Menno but with a certain derision because of a sudden she thought, surprising herself, *The truth is that nothing is everlasting. Not the stars nor the mountains. Not the martyrs' sayings nor their hymns, nor the Amish,* she thought. *Nor faith nor science or art. Not even love.*

For hadn't Freida's love put Lawrence into cement? There he stood fixed forever. But not, surely, everlasting. Only separated alike from dissolution and becoming, he hung like the bug in Papa's amber paperweight, a species, said Papa, which had remained fixed and unchanging for a million years.

Of a sudden Dorsey felt weary to her soul. She wanted to leave but found that Menno had persuaded the caretaker to unlock the cabin and show him the furniture Lawrence had fashioned with his own hands.

She watched him examine each piece carefully, taking a professional interest, discussing its merits and flaws with the caretaker who was, like Menno, something of a master carpenter. As with the college student and Lawrence's writing, Dorsey gathered they held a low opinion of Lawrence's carpentry.

Driving down the hill, Dorsey said to Menno, "He was like the martyrs. Although he was opposed by many, he held to his beliefs."

But Menno said, "His furniture wasn't plum. And his nails," Menno added, "were badly driven."

Yet he knew that life evolves, thought Dorsey. *And he believed in freedom and hope and love. And though he suffered, he recanted neither love nor hope nor freedom nor evolving.*

That night in bed, Dorsey pictured, with her last waking thought, how O'Keeffe must have looked, painting her canvas under the tree. She imagined the artist lying on her back looking up through black branches toward the light of the pale and distant stars.

When Dorsey fell asleep at last, she slept soundly all through the dark hours. It wasn't until morning, after they had returned the rental car and breakfasted on hotcakes and bacon that she realized what she must do with Papa's ashes.

— 16 —

If Menno was amazed to learn that Dorsey wanted to continue on to the Pacific Ocean, he was downright alarmed to hear that she wished to cover the remaining distance by plane. She confessed to a great feeling of urgency. An overpowering need to see her task quickly completed.

The prospect of leaving the earth, of rising into the air unmanned him. It shook him to his shoe soles. Yet how could he leave her now the journey was so nearly at an end?

"When I've scattered Papa's ashes, we'll go back to Captina on the train," Dorsey promised. "We'll be home in three days' time."

And they began to talk together about Captina, and he thought how the ride home would be a long, sweet ride and worth the trouble of this brief flight.

However, once he'd entered the airport, Menno began to feel, in some deep irredeemable way, a dark tide of horror rising in him. He began to look about him and to ask himself, over and over, *What am I, Menno Yoder, doing in this unclean place?*

Dorsey returned from the ticket counter to find Menno shaking.

"What is it?" she asked him.

He said that his stomach pained him. When, over the loudspeaker, their flight was announced, she began to draw him toward the flight gate.

"Come on!" she said. But he held back, twisting his arm out of her grasp.

The flight was announced again.

She held out her hand toward him, but he took a step back. And then another. And didn't speak. Or couldn't speak. When she took his hand, he let her lead him three steps toward the gate. Then he pulled away once again and stood, wide-eyed, his face gone very pale.

What Dorsey thought was this: *He's as he was when we climbed the tree.*

And she knew he would never get on the airplane. And he knew.

"Take the train back to Captina," she said. "In a few days, I'll meet you there."

She slung the satchel over her shoulder. Through the canvas, she could feel the edge of the funerary box resting along her thigh.

*

People around them were saying their farewells.

She hesitated, wanting him to come. They called the flight.

Dorsey looked at Menno standing there in his barn-door pants and his galoshes and his flat, broad-brimmed hat. And she thought she wouldn't go. But when the plane was called for the last time, she turned away and was carried along by the boarding passengers up the tunnel and onto the plane.

— 17 —

Almost as soon as she sat down in her seat, the plane began to move. It swung around onto the runway and picked up speed. Dorsey leaned her forehead against the window, straining her eyes but she couldn't see Menno.

Then, with a surge of power like a horse breaking into a gallop, the plane leaped free of the earth and entered the sky.

Looking down, Dorsey saw the many-colored country spread out beneath her like a woven tapestry. She glimpsed rock mesas, swept into strange shapes by the wind and the great canyon carved by the fast-running Colorado River. Somewhere, far to the east, lay Captina.

And now, far below, was the white patch of the atomic proving ground. Then the watershed, the continental divide, the wrinkles of land that were the Rocky Mountains. Ahead, to the west, was the black ooze of the LeBrea Tar Pits and beyond them, the blue-green rise and fall of the Pacific.

For a time Dorsey had a heady feeling of freedom as she rode high above the earth. Sometimes, when white streaks obscured her downward view, she thought, *I am above the clouds!* But then she remembered how Menno had said, "No matter how far out you go into space, or how long you travel in time, you get no closer heaven." And she understood that journeys were of different sorts, and she thought of the moon shot and of Christ walking the Jerico Road.

*

It was evening when the plane landed in Santa Ana. By the time Dorsey rented a car and drove to Newport Beach, night had come, and a full moon shone on the sand. People had kindled driftwood in rubber tires laid on the beach and were cooking their suppers beside the ocean.

She walked down across the shingle to land's end where a rising tide lapped at the shore, then out a ways into the Pacific so that the water, warmish and salty, washed over her ankles. She waited until a cloud veiled the moon. Then she opened the funerary box. Holding it aloft at arm's length, she turned it upside down.

The sea wind caught up her father's ashes and flung them high and spread them wide so that they sifted down like snowflakes into the waves. She tossed the box into the ocean.

Afterward, she walked slowly back up the strand, her shoes sloshing, and stood at the outer edge of light thrown by a fire where a bearded boy and a girl with yellow hair were roasting hotdogs. Dorsey moved an inch closer, trying to warm herself. Her wet pantlegs, her shirttail and her hair fluttered in the brisk, briny wind.

The couple, beckoning her closer, handed her a hotdog on a paper plate. The wiener, blackened and split, lay sizzling on its bun. When she bit into it, the juice ran down her chin. She ate it hungrily and afterward threw the plate into the fire where it clenched itself into a red fist, then fell open like a dark flower, blooming.

— 18 —

When the strawberries ripened, Dorsey worked at the picking. And after that, at gathering flowers for seed. And then in various vegetable harvests.

Now and again, as she continued on from job to job, she visualized her father's desk with the notes for his unfinished biography of Lawrence spread across it. Or, in her mind's eye, she saw Menno: his barndoor pants and his Dutch Boy haircut. And she told herself, *Tomorrow I'll buy a ticket to Captina.* Or she thought, *the day after tomorrow.* It happened, however, that her life offered many unexpected turnings so that for the first time, she began to follow paths of her own choosing. In the end, Captina all but faded from her memory, and her days with Menno became as exotic and remote as the tales her papa had used to tell about his boyhood on Grandma Bendlers' farm.

— 19 —

In Captina, two years after the World, Logan Bendler, died, his house was sold for back taxes. The next spring Menno married Naomi and went to farming his father-in-law's land. During the summer, with the help of the People, the young couple raised a dwelling and a barn on the west division of the farm and Menno began to bid in livestock at auction.

Their children, when they came, were well-grown and comely.

Menno was content with his life. There were times, however, in bed beside Naomi, when he felt he lay immobile at the bottom of a wide, dark lake while, high above, bright wings passed over him bound for some far off shore.

The Lost Book

Emory

The subject of the lecture was, "Impotence: Remedies, New and Old."

Emory hadn't wanted to come.

"I'm done with that foolishness," he'd told Floris, his wife. Meaning sex. He'd said he was resigned though regretful to bid his libido *adieu*.

Floris hadn't found this funny. A credulous little woman who hung on with the grip of a bulldog to her notion that miracles were performed and prayers answered, she'd urged him to attend the talk. "It might be you'll get restored," Floris had said.

These were the early days of Viagra's appearance on the scene, and Emory who, on principle resisted anything new, had a bad feeling about the whole subject.

Only after he agreed to make the drive over to Stafford did Floris tell him she wouldn't be accompanying him. This was her excuse: she had to search for a lost book.

Thin-sounding, thought Emory. Yet if you knew how Flory felt about this particular book, maybe not.

"I can't stop looking," said Floris, "until I've found it."

*

The lecturer was a prominent urologist, Dr. Roscoe Booker. By a quarter to four, at least 80 people were crowded into a room built to hold 50. The metal folding chairs, scrunched together in tight rows, were, every one, taken and people standing three-deep along the back wall.

The audience was mostly older men. Although, looking over the crowd, Emory was able to pick out a woman here, a woman there. Wives come with their husbands. On a small table in the center aisle, a slide projector with a carousel had been set up.

"Lights out," said Dr. Booker, and Emory found himself, along with the rest of the audience, in the dark.

First, the doctor projected a few cartoons to put everyone at ease. One slide showed a man getting a penile transplant from a horse. In another, a couple lay in bed, the woman playing a flute at the man's tool hoping to coax it up as was done with snakes in India. As they all sat looking at this, someone snickered. Emory judged it was a woman.

After the cartoons, came slides of what Dr. Booker called "old cures." A man sticking a needle into his member. Another man poking a pill down *his*. A fellow placing *his* into a tube attached to a battery-driven suction pump.

Emory noticed how the tops of these pictures were, every one, cut off so you never saw above the men's shoulders and couldn't help wondering what sort of look they'd got on their faces whilst they were doing these things to themselves.

Of course, everyone was waiting for the low-down on the little blue pill, but Dr. Booker was saving the best for last.

Two men appeared in the doorway, bringing more chairs. Emory watched them set these up behind the back row. A scramble ensued in which those lucky enough to get a chair, sat. The rest resumed their standing positions.

All these old men, Emory thought, *wanting to get back their hairy goats' legs. Wanting to be Great God Pans again! Not only hopeless,* Emory judged it, *but ridiculous.* Picturing such a happening, however, he felt a stir down in his own lap. Or thought he did.

Dr. Booker's secretary handed around packets of printed material, each stapled in the upper right corner. Small and fair, she resembled Floris somewhat. Floris when she was younger. About the time their children were in high school. Whenever Floris had walked past him in those days, up it stood. *Ten-hut!*

Nights in their marriage bed they'd spun and leaped. Rocked, meshed together like the branches they'd seen sweeping down the Niagara River on their wedding trip.

They lay yet in that self-same bed, sleeping now the light sleep of the elderly. Or, wakeful in the quiet, childless house, they turned in the night, easing their joints. They got up in the dark to pee. Neither of them dreamt much anymore. Or else they forgot their dreams.

And so that morning as they'd shut off the alarm and raised the window blinds, they hadn't discussed dreams but the lecture. Floris had reiterated her expectations that Emory might regain his youthful vigor. She had said to him, "Remember the way it was?"

"Of course, I remember!" he snapped since small good *that* did him.

What he'd thought was this: *Floris reads too many books*. "You don't face reality," he told her. "You don't dwell in the actual world with the rest of us."

"I do!" she said, coloring.

The upshot was they'd parted with their tail feathers ruffled.

*

After breakfast, Emory had gone to Mrs. Hopgood's to fix her kitchen sink. When he returned, Floris, bent on patching things up, said, "I'll bake you an elderberry pie for supper."

He hadn't answered her, since, though it shouldn't have done, this ruffled him further. It was her pity he couldn't put up with. And her female solution: *Give the lad a sweet and he'll forget his broken toy*. So, he'd spurned her pie. Afterwards he wished he'd been kinder.

Everybody has their losses, he'd thought. And in many ways Flory's loss was a good deal worse than his. Not the loss of her pet book, but of her sister who had died just after the first of the year. Floris couldn't seem to bring herself to accept it that Neva was gone.

— 2 —

Floris

The morning of the lecture, as soon as Emory collected his plumbing tools and backed his truck out the drive, Floris, still in her woolly robe and pink slippers, searched the house, every cranny and nook. She looked on each of the stair steps and under the bed. In the closets and cupboards and drawers.

She had to admit she might have lost the book anywhere. She'd got into the habit of carrying it around with her. It had been the only thing that gave her comfort after Neva's passing.

Floris never looked to miss her sister the way she did. Because, truth to tell, she and Neva had had their squabbles. Sometimes they'd tramped on one another's feelings so hard they could scarce bring themselves to exchange more than a nod for weeks afterward.

Neva was like the Tones, their mama's people: down-to-earth. A no-nonsense woman. Floris, on the other hand, took after their papa's kin, the Sheridans, who were, every one of them, mush-headed romantics. Small wonder they seldom saw eye-to-eye.

If she were to count their differences, Floris judged she'd need all her fingers and most of her toes. Take size, to begin with. An egret had bigger bones than Floris. Neva was a size 44. Solid as sacked sugar and lofty as an oak, that was Neva.

Their opinions were as opposite as their measurements. If Floris said 'top,' Neva said 'bottom.' If Floris said 'stop,' Neva said 'go.' Besides which, Neva was a non-believer while Floris was Pentecostal. The bitterest of their quarrels came from this or anyway the one that hurt the most. The one that, somehow or other, seemed to be going on yet.

Because the bickering between them didn't stop when Neva died. Only the location changed. It moved inside Floris' head.

"Neva's gone to glory," she remarked to Emory soon after the burying. "She's up in heaven singing with the angels."

I'm not, came Neva's voice from somewhere in Floris' brain. *I am out here in White Oak Cemetery under a ton and a half of dirt!*

But your soul's in heaven, Floris told her, without moving her lips.

Every bit of me, said Neva, *is right here.*

It was on this self-same day that the grief over Neva's death had intensified and commenced to squeeze Floris' heart like an iron fist.

*

The book-search proving futile, Floris dressed, ran a comb through her hair and knotted it up. Quickly smoothing the bedclothes, she drew up the spread. In former times, making love in the night, she and Emory had used to kick the quilts galley-west so that straightening the bed was an all-morning chore. Floris smiled, remembering. *God knows,* thought Floris, *I never begrudged the time.*

In his younger days her husband had been an uncommonly vigorous lover. And a prodigious worker, strong in his back and his arms. As to character, he'd got what in books was called 'valor.' It ran deep in him like a granite core. You hit it whenever you had to do with Emory. There it was, every time. It never crumbled. Wherever he went in the world, he carried it with him. Or he'd used to. *You were ever the rock I rested on: Emory,* Floris thought.

On their wedding trip, when she first heard the roar of the great falls, it frightened her. It was like immense drums beating beneath the world's rim and, listening to it, her knees shook under her. So loud and continuous it was, so violent and destructive, she had turned away, afraid to look.

Emory put his arm around her and so, after all, she looked. The water was moving fast and dropping down heavily, ton after ton, as if the sky itself were falling, but Floris was no longer fearful since he wasn't.

How could it be then that he was so ready to let old age beat him? Why did he cave in so easily these days to life's "slings and arrows" as she'd read in *Hamlet*. "Keep trying," she always told him. "Don't give up. Don't be like Neva."

Yet here she was, she, her own self, so disheartened by the loss of a book that she began to feel ready to let Neva win their last argument. To feel that she must, after all, let her sister disappear into death.

For a brief time after Neva's passing, the busy-work of the funeral had kept Floris too occupied to grieve: the selecting of Neva's casket and her vault-lining along with which dress to lay her out in. (She'd chosen the navy with polka dots and the Peter Pan collar.) And, of course, feeding all those people. All those Tones and all those Sheridans. They didn't get through the meal without the usual fistfight.

Liam Sheridan hit Harry Tone in the eye with his fist, though what it was over, Floris couldn't say. Something political, she thought. Something harking back to the New Deal and having to do with pigs.

Afterward, as first the January then the February cold reached into her blood, she'd begun to feel the weight of Neva's loss laid across her shoulders like a load of stones. Every breath she drew hurt her.

When, week by week, Floris kept to the house, Emory commenced worrying at her. Coaxing her to go to garage sales or to Bingo at the church. But before she could try either the one or the other, her friend, Marie Hale, had, about the middle of March, sent her a book which she'd got on inter-library loan from the Malaga College Library in Robertsville. Its title was, *The Novel, A Modern Guide to Fifteen English Masterpieces.* The author was Elizabeth A. Drew.

Floris soon discovered that reading in this book was like dabbing cloves on a toothache. The pain was still there only not so sharp. A body could catch her breath. Snatch a little sleep of a night. Even go out into the world again.

The pity was that this moment of respite didn't last. A calamity happened. Floris lost the book. One minute she had it in her hand, the next it was gone.

After failing to find it in the house the morning of the lecture, Floris thought, *Then I lost it in Captina.* She decided to drive downtown that afternoon and retrace every step she'd taken the day before.

— 3 —
Emory

"We never expected so many," Dr. Booker said into the microphone, making it whine, startling the audience. He was beginning his talk, Emory noted, at 4 P.M. sharp just as advertised.

Dr. Roscoe Booker's being a urologist made Emory grin, because it reminded him how the Good Lord would have His joke, putting the fount of life at the pissing site.

Most of a person's sex life was just that ridiculous. For instance, he and Floris made love for the first time in a cemetery. He was 16, she was 15. They'd laid themselves down in a grassy hollow soft as any bed. Though he hadn't minded, the nearby graves put Flory off somewhat.

In the lecture room a few of the people were sipping coffee from Styrofoam cups. There was a machine in the lobby. The room was in a Holiday Inn in the town of Stafford, twenty some miles west of Emory's and Floris' home village of Captina.

Of a sudden, squeezing past him, a man stepped on Emory's foot. Inside his shoe he felt his sock split against the nail of his big toe. What he thought was this: *It's high time I gave my toenails a trim.*

Even after Dr. Booker had begun his talk, the old men kept coming in. Caucasian and Afro-American. Hispanic and Asian. Some in three-piece suits, pale and scholarly with pince-nez and trimmed beards. Others showing the rough skin of men who spent their time mostly out-of-doors. Some sported woolly berets set rakish on the fronts of their heads. Others wore caps with logos. Most had hair, white or grey, although a good number had bald pates. Fat, thin. Tall, short. But every one with anxious eyes. Embarrassed but hopeful.

All during the slides, the white-collar men cracked wise. The blue-collars just sat there with their jaws dropped down.

Some of these last Emory judged to be roofers or construction workers. Or maybe they laid sewer tile. These were men who labored with their hands. *Like me,* thought Emory. *I've done all them jobs and more.*

His name, "Emory," meant "king of work." *And God knows I'm that,* he told himself. *If ever I climb the golden stairs,* he thought, *and St. Peter breaks open my soul like a fortune cookie, he'll find these words, "Like the fool he was, he worked hisself to death."*

Floris' name meant "to bloom." She did, too. Not so much with beauty these days as with kindness. With caring. *Ask our children,* thought Emory. *And our grandchildren. Ask our neighbors. Ask the strangers she's forever helping along their ways. As for her husband,* he thought. *Just use your eyes. I'm living proof.* Well-fed, he was and, for the most part, contented. They were good companions, he and Floris. Good lovers, too. Or they used to be.

As he listened to Dr. Booker speak about each of the slides, Emory wondered if the other old men found these projected cures as unsettling as he did. For instance, when Dr. B. explained how you put an elastic ring round your member to keep it pumped up, he'd thought of how, as a small boy, he'd wound a rubber-band onto his finger so tight it turned blue and pretty nearly dropped off. Under present conditions, this memory made him squirm.

An erection that wouldn't go down, according to Dr. Booker, was called 'Priapism,' named for Priapus, a Greek god whom, unlike Pan, none of them wanted to emulate. At least to this degree. Once the tool of a man he'd injected with a combination of two drugs remained rigid for four days, the doc told them, and every man in the room turned pale.

— 4 —

Floris

As soon as Emory left for the lecture, Floris put on her brown sweater. She went out into the garage and poked her fingers into the folds of the Desoto's seats and, using a flashlight, peered under the dashboard. She took up the rubber mats and gave them a shake. She emptied the glove compartment, though she never would have put there the *Elizabeth Drew*, as she came to name it.

She ransacked the garage and, in the yard, felt amongst the new grasses, wet from last night's rain. No book.

Several hours after lunch, at about the time Emory's lecture was beginning, Floris, dressed now in a light jacket with a babushka tied under her chin, arrived in downtown Captina. She parked in front of Al's, the restaurant where she'd had her lunch the day before. She checked the booth she'd sat in. For the briefest of moments she thought, catching her breath, that she saw the book lying on the far edge of the seat. But it was only a shadow cast by the table top.

She examined Al's Lost and Found, a cardboard box slid under the coat rack. She spoke to the waitress who had served her and then to Al, himself. No one remembered finding a book. No book had been turned in. Floris felt like bawling.

Only Emory guessed how much the book meant to her. And even he didn't understand why. She scarcely did herself. All she knew was that the reason had to do with Neva. With winning this last argument between them.

Back when Floris started working as lay assistant at the Captina Library, she'd commenced reading what they had there. Reading anything. Reading everything. After a while, she'd settled on novels. Soon she was sorting out the 'deep' ones from the piddling ones. Marie Hale, who'd been librarian in Captina forever, helped her choose.

Sometimes Flory understood what an author was getting at, sometimes she didn't. But before long she did see that the best of them put forth answers to life's questions in a way similar to what the Bible did, only, it might be not so holy.

When Marie leant her *Elizabeth Drew,* she felt she'd been given the key to the castle. Because on page after page this learned woman told, in plain *understandable* words, exactly what the authors were getting at in their deep books.

Floris left Al's and moved about Captina, retracing her steps of the day before. The drycleaners. The grocery. The courthouse where she'd bought a dog license for Bugle, Emory's old hunting hound. Walking the main drag, she studied the sidewalks and the street. Now and again, she stopped this person or that and asked after the book. Not one of them had seen it.

Floris turned down Bartell Street, peering into shop windows. The sun glanced off the glass making it hard to see the displays. One store, selling art supplies, had a number of watercolor paintings by local artists set up on easels.

Once the Captina library had sponsored an art show featuring local talent. To make their pictures, the artists had used fragments of real objects glued onto boards or dangling from string. Floris remembered one display that featured a single shoe. One glove. Two candle sticks, one containing a candle, one empty. A ring with the stone missing. And a doll's arm. The piece was entitled, "Loss."

The arm belonged to a Barbie Doll, judging by the size. At the time these ordinary items made into art had struck her as amusing. Now the thought of them, especially the arm, made her want to weep.

Floris returned home feeling defeated. Her bones ached from so much walking. She telephoned Al's several times during the afternoon. No book had been turned in. Each call she made was like a door closing.

As the day wore on, she began to picture a loutish busser of dishes throwing the *Elizabeth Drew* into a bin of garbage. A maintenance man sweeping it out the door. Or, she thought, a thief could have *stolen* the book. Slipped it under his or her coat and carried it away to keep or to sell.

Now, glancing through the window, she saw Bugle chewing on the garden hose. Since the village had passed an ordinance that dogs must be confined, he spent his days chained to a stake. He'd worn the grass off a part of the lawn by dragging the chain back and forth. Floris, sweaterless this time, went to move the hose out of his reach.

— 5 —
Emory

After the slides, there was an intermission during which the ladies' auxiliary from the hospital served home-made cookies, tea and coffee.

Cheering us up with sweets, thought Emory, mindful of the elderberry pie. But he took two cookies, one oatmeal, one peanut butter, and drank a cup of decaf java.

Standing about amongst people who were chatting and eating put him in mind of the reunions Flory's kinfolks, the Sheridans, had used to host when he and Floris were courting. The second Tuesday in July each year, there'd been a family dinner. All the Sheridans from miles around gathered. Long tables were set up out-of-doors. He remembered the white cloths and the rows of plates. Never such an abundance of food. Never such feasting seen on this earth! Everyone managing to eat and talk at once.

Each woman brought the dish she was famous for. Flory's Aunt Lilah made her lima bean casserole. Cousin Gert made current tarts. Everyone bragged on the food. After the meal, the women traded recipes, dress patterns and news of betrothals, weddings, births and funerals. The children ran about with flushed faces and sweaty hair. The men talked mileage. Got out maps and showed how they'd come, how they were going back.

*

Up and down the hall in the Holiday Inn, companies pushing certain of the cures had set up posters and their agents were distributing literature and giving spiels.

One firm was represented by a pretty, young thing with fried hair and a brief skirt. Emory, like most of the others, was too embarrassed to approach her.

The fact was that most of the men talked, not to salespersons, but to each other. They spoke about their hobbies. About sports. About dry-walling and 4-versus 6-cylinder engines. One group discussed hunting.

"I shot the lead duck," said a deep-voiced fellow, "and then I shot four more further back in the V. My dog fetched me every one. I wouldn't take," bragged the man, "a thousand dollars for that dog. He's got a Velcro mouth. Never drops what he picks up, never leaves a mark on it."

At once Emory thought of Bugle. No hunting dog that ever lived could match Bugle in his prime. A bay like a tolling bell. Fleet of foot and a peerless nose. Part Blue Tick, part Redbone. A dab of bloodhound, too, to judge by that wrinkled forehead. They had treed many a coon together, he and Bugle.

Grew old together, too. Bugle was gray about the muzzle now as Emory was above the ears. Man and dog, their sight and hearing weren't what they had been.

Giving up hunting was hard on Bugle. He pined after it. *Like us old men pine after nooky*, Emory thought. At night Emory sometimes dreamed that he and Floris were going at it in the old way. Bugle dreamed of hunting. As he lay stretched on the floor, asleep, you'd see his paws move as if he were running. Sometimes he gave out a few muffled yips deep in his throat, without ever opening his mouth.

The lights blinked to call everyone back into the lecture room. The Auxiliary Ladies began to gather up the cups and plates and pack the left-over cookies into tins. Bustling, heavy-set women, most of them, were dressed in flowered prints with aprons tied around their waists. If she were alive and dwelling in Stafford, Neva would be among them, Emory thought. Hippering here, hurrying there, her hair curling moist and fine about her little ears, her broad face growing red and redder. But for all the heat engendered by motion, her eyes would have their same cold, jelled look. Would resemble pieces of black ice. *The name 'Neva'*, thought Emory, *means 'snow'*.

Snow storm, more like, he mused. Neva had ever been a mover and a doer. She met life head on. Met it as a hammer meets a nail. As goats butt heads. She never backed off.

Born earlier, she'd have been a suffragette. In the Sixties she carried signs, joined marches and sit-ins against war, segregation and the destruction of the environment. Maybe, Emory speculated, it was because no better world emerged as they'd all believed it would, that she'd settled into her stark, bitter view of life.

Emory missed Neva. Not as much as Floris did, but enough. She'd been good for him. She'd kept his mind shaken up. Kept him on his toes. She'd been good for Flory, as well. A dreamer needs somebody around to, now and again, pull her back to earth. And God knows, Neva'd had enough reality-facing grit for all of them.

Her entire life she'd stared into the abyss and never blinked. She was content to do, as best she could, what each day demanded of her without glancing back nor striving to see ahead. For her, the present moment was enough.

It's true that, as the years passed, she began to wonder where, when and how her death would come on her. As a result of this intense curiosity, her face took on an expectant, apprehensive look.

*

After the break, Emory sat in a different chair, one toward the middle of the room. He sat behind a couple who, while somewhat younger than the rest, were yet well past middle-age. They were a dressy pair. *Like the men and women you see in magazines aimed at the elderly*, thought Emory. The woman wore a pink polyester pants-suit. She colored her hair blonde and her ear-bobs were the dangling sort. The man was sporty in a Fair Isle sweater.

When Dr. Booker tapped the microphone to bring the crowd to order, the man laid his arm along his wife's shoulders as if the two of them were at the movies and the main film starting up.

Inappropriate, Emory thought. Then admitted this was probably just sour grapes. Truth to tell he resented them for facing their loss shoulder to shoulder while he sat here alone because Floris was searching for her idiot book.

Dr. B. took off his coat and rolled his sleeves up to the elbow.

"Like a preacher," a man near Emory observed, "getting ready to coax us into the amen corner."

Which, Emory supposed, was where they belonged. *Because what they all mourned was no longer sharing in the creative force. Not Pan's* he thought, *nor Priapus'. Floris' God's, perhaps.*

— 6 —
Floris

Floris, having saved the hose from Bugle's gnawing, stood stock still at the edge of the garden rubbing her eyes. Because of a sudden she seemed to see her sister in her accustomed spot under the pear tree.

So often at this time of day, around 5 of an afternoon, Neva used to sit on the wooden bench, dappled with sun, snapping beans or shelling peas. *Here she sits again*, Floris thought. *Or her spirit sits here, freed from the grave.*

But, of course, it was an optical illusion. A trick of light and shadow playing on the split-bottom basket that leaned against the spade handle.

Rolling the hose onto its spool, Floris mused how, since the burying, she'd felt herself closer to Neva in the garden than in any other place. Now that the weather had commenced warming, she often carried her books out to the bench.

During the dead of each winter, Floris had been accustomed to draw up a garden plan.

"The Salinas Valley," Neva would say, peering over her shoulder.

And, of course, Neva was right. The real garden would of necessity turn out a great deal smaller and more jumbled. Less symmetrical. And the more exotic of the seeds she ordered usually refused to grow at all.

Emory did the planting. Floris was hopeless at that part. Neva and Floris tended the plants, gathered in the harvest, canned or froze it. Floris, with her mind ever on her books, was, in all respects, poor help. So said Neva. And, of course, it was true.

"Wake up, Floris," Neva would rap out, shoving a pan of tomatoes into her solar plexus. "Come out of the clouds!"

*

The wet grass and Bugle's muddy paws reminded Floris of last night's storm. Floris and Emory had climbed out of their bed and stood at the window watching the wind toss the pear tree's branches and flatten the jonquils along the hedge.

Their house, the old Sheridan homestead, stood on the east edge of Captina, their bedroom windows overlooking a few acres of tilled land to the west, all that remained of the farm.

In the lightning flashes they saw rain pounding the dark soil.

"Like horses galloping," said Emory, who was often reminded of horses, his father being once a driver, then trainer of standard-breds.

Gazing over that field always caused Floris to think of *her* father as well. Of the many evenings she'd heard him coming in off the land, singing. A small, broad man, he was. Red-headed, with a powerful tenor voice.

As he drove home the cattle, he sang about the bold Fenian men. The pikes that gathered at the rising of the moon. And about the wind that shook the barley while lovers stood too near the edge of battle. "On my breast in blood she died," he sang and when he stepped through the kitchen door, his eyes were teary.

Their mother would laugh at him over her shoulder, her arms floury from biscuit dough. And Neva laughed. But Floris was filled with yearning. With a sense of personal loss as if she herself had lived in that faraway land and left it behind as the older Sheridans had: the green hills and the peat bogs, the cottages in the mist, the rocky roads and the fairies. The hunger and the passion, the heroic wars and the holy martyrs.

Since Emory wasn't here to give Bugle his walk, Floris took pity on the old dog and turned him loose of his chain for a bit. She watched him lope about the yard, sniffing amongst the bushes, the joy of freedom in his every move.

Rain water stood puddled in the driveway and in the garden. She picked up the basket and set it on the bench to dry out. Then she resumed her search for *Elizabeth Drew*. She moved the tools about on Emory's shelf in the shed, then poked about in the plastic bags of trash set against the back wall, shifting them, one by one so as to peer underneath.

During February, Floris had packed Neva's dresses into bags like these. Her sweaters. Her shoes. Her blue winter coat, nearly new. The Salvation Army had come on February 20th and taken them away.

Most of Neva's clothes were hand-made. It had been their habit, the two sisters, during the cold months, to occupy their time with stitching together dresses for themselves on their mother's old Singer. And they made shirts for Emory. Their mother had taught them to sew.

She'd been a talented seamstress who'd come to Captina as a girl, living now in one household, now another, sewing for the families. She stitched crinoline dresses like the blooms of flowers and cotton petticoats edged in eyelet lace. Her quilts lay yet on most of the beds in Captina. On the mayor's bed. On Marie Hale's. And on Floris and Emory's.

She could patch scraps and wisps into beguiling patterns. So could their dad, except instead of bedcovers he made tunes that, like birdsong, dissolved on the air. She'd lost her sight at the last, their poor mama. Too much sewing, some said. Others said it was a disease brought on by age. Floris used to hold her own eyes shut trying to discover what blindness was like. And never a clue until she'd come across a book of Milton's verses. "O dark, dark, dark/ Amid the blaze of noon," she'd read, and, "Irrevocably dark/ Total eclipse/ Without all hope of day!" Then she'd known.

Along with clothes, Floris and Neva had worked at items for the Captina Ladies' Club bazaars. Floris crocheted doilies, filmy white circlets, light as air. Neva hooked rugs. She left one unfinished. It lay yet in the corner of the kitchen, partially basted together, the edges of the rags beginning to ravel.

As Floris stepped out of the shed, she heard Bugle giving tongue. There he went, racing across the field, nose to the ground. She whistled after him, using her fingers, but he paid her no heed.

"Bugle!" she shrieked. "You, Bugle!"

When he came at last it was in his own good time. Of a sudden here he was trotting toward her slowly, carrying some small thing in his mouth.

He laid it at her feet, and she saw it was a young rabbit, its neck broken, its head lolling down. The fur of its belly was wet from the dog's saliva, its skin flayed and bloody.

Age has taken away your gentle mouth, Floris thought, *as it took away my mother's sight, Neva's hope and Emory's manhood.*

She lifted the spade and dug a trench in the parrot tulip bed. Still warm, the rabbit was, when she laid it in the hole. Pulling dirt over it, she twisted down the stem of a tulip. As it straightened, two white petals dropped onto the mound. *These are the tears of God*, Floris thought, *who mourns for sparrows. And for rabbits.*

— 7 —

Emory

As the afternoon wore on, Dr. Booker spoke ever more rapidly into the microphone, his pleasant, vibrant voice rolling out sentence after sentence full of medical-sounding words. Most of the words had to do with the male organ.

"Flaccid," said Dr. Booker. "Tumescent. Rigid. Spongy. Engorged."

Emory found his mind wandering. His thoughts, thinning like water vapor, seemed to drift slowly upward and condense on the glass covers of the ceiling lights.

He shifted his weight and drew his right calf over his left thigh. He narrowed his gaze, concentrating it on the urologist's teeth, appearing, disappearing behind his lips as he spoke.

Dr. B. was examining various causes of impotence. There were a good many, both separate and in combination.

"You have your psychological causes," said the doctor. "One poor fellow, every time he was in the mood, there stood his girlfriend's Siamese cat, growling, at the foot of the bed."

The Fair Isle man snorted and slapped his wife on the back, leading Emory to believe they kept cats.

"Stress," said Dr. Booker. "Anxiety. Family or job-related. On the physical side," he continued, "you have your vascular disease, your arterial sclerosis, MS, blood pressure medication, diabetes, prostate surgery. Pelvic injuries," he said. "Alcoholism. Low hormone level.

"Before we decide which procedure to recommend," the doctor said, "we run checks on your glucose, cholesterol and testosterone. And we ask you questions: "Do you wake up in the morning with an erection?" ("I should be so lucky!" someone said.)

The audience, Emory noticed, was inviting itself into the lecture. "When was the last time you had a normal erection?" ("When was the Johnstown Flood?") "When was your last satisfactory intercourse?" ("Satisfactory to who?") Emory looked around the room. This last was a woman's voice. "We test your nerve and blood vessel function. And we evaluate your alcohol consumption."

A chilled beer on a summer evening, a glass of wine, now and again, with a meal (two of life's most agreeable pleasures), that was all Emory ever took. He left the hard stuff alone. Flory's father, of course, had been an alcoholic. His own dad, to please Emory's mother, had been teetotal.

In truth, Emory's dad hadn't cared what he ate or drank, as long as he'd got horses about him. Even the family took second place. Often when Emory looked into his father's eyes, he'd imagined he saw horses running across their dark centers. Horses pulling sulkies.

Emory himself cared about horses, but in a different way. He didn't have his father's need to touch them, nor to spend every waking hour working with them. Though he'd no religion to speak of, Emory supposed what he felt toward horses was a sort of reverence.

Because of his father's profession, Emory grew up around stables and racetracks. Watching horses run, he'd thought their skin lovely, the way it winked and dimpled as the muscles moved underneath. When they galloped, loose in the fields, their manes and tails rippled and snapped like pieces of silk cloth. Their colors were, some of them, so deep and bright they'd stopped his breath. Earth tones. And hues of the night: bluish-blacks and silvers.

But there were other animals and even birds and fish he liked as much and in the same way. For their elegance and their natural grace in motion. Their grit and humor. Their strength and canniness and joy.

He'd felt almost the same toward certain landscapes. Lusty, upward-reaching mountains and hills. Mystery-ridden hollows and calm sun-lit valleys. Falling water, always the same, always different. Rivers and lakes, bright above, dark below. Endless green-grey oceans, lacy with churnings. As he'd watched their salty, restless waves roll toward the shore, then draw away, Emory had been reminded of people falling in and out of love.

He recalled standing on land so flat he'd felt himself circled by the world's rim, feet grounded in dirt and rock, poll pressing against the sun. Once, walking on ice as blue as the veins in a man's arm, he'd turned giddy with wonder. Felt wonder, too, treading on islands set in the sea like the thick, dark heads of bathing giants.

Emory had traveled a great deal by the time he married Floris. And he and Floris had traveled. Now that old age was coming on him, he went nowhere to speak of. He was uneasy away from home. Strange but true.

Strange, too, that landscapes, even animals and birds seemed to be less vital now, less wondrous. It was as if a film had formed over his eyes.

"You're giving up on life is what it is," said Floris. "Don't. Hang on!"

*

Dr. Booker, speaking now in a kind of singsong, was going back over the slides, explaining how each cure operated, indicating the advantages and drawbacks. He spent a long time describing one cure not shown on the slides, a surgically implanted device, semi-rigid, which could be inflated with fluid. "We have," he said, "a two-piece design and a three-piece design."

"I'd feel part-man part-hardware!" said a deep voice behind Emory. It was the man with the remarkable hunting dog. Emory wondered would the prosthesis corrode if a body sat on it of a rainy morning in a duck blind.

"Now as to *Viagra*," said Dr. Booker. All ears perked up.

— 8 —

Floris

While burying the rabbit, Floris lost track of Bugle. Like the book, one minute her eye was on him, the next he had disappeared. Looping the chain over her arm, she set off across a plowed field in search of the hound.

The soaked soil clung to her shoes and tripped her up so that she began to keep to the left edge of the field where weeds and long grasses made the ground firmer.

She hoped Bugle hadn't gone down into Captina. If he had, the village marshal was sure to catch him and lock him up, in which case a fine would be forthcoming and Emory would be cross.

She'd got a far piece over the field when she heard Bugle on the hill ahead. It was nothing like the ringing bay of his youth, but she knew his voice right enough. He'd cornered something up in the old Sheridan Cemetery.

The sky was overcast. It might be more rain would fall. The wind had risen and it pulled at her hair as she started to climb, carrying off a pin, loosening the coil.

When she'd nearly reached the top of the hill, Floris stood still to catch her breath and to gaze out across the countryside. Up above, oak trees spread their ancient branches over the Sheridan graves. Floris' grandmother and grandfather were here. Her great-grandparents. Her uncles and her aunts. Her mother and her dad. And of course, Neva.

Below stood the house and, beyond it, small and linear, Captina. Above the roofs of the village, a steeple poked up into the sky: the Ebenezer Church. Her church. A comforting sight, Floris thought. But from up the hill Neva said, *Not to me!*

Nor, when she was living, had the Bible comforted Neva as it did Floris. For inspiration Neva read self-help and Robert Ingersol.

In her mind's eye, Floris pictured her sister in her later years, her graying hair like flame fallen to ash, sitting on the garden bench with her favorite Ingersol volume, *Why I am An Agnostic*, spread out across her knees.

Neva had caught Ingersol like a disease from a favorite uncle who'd thought it dashing, while attending college, to play at being a non-believer. He'd got over it, but Neva never had. When Floris was baptized into the Ebenezers, Neva had quoted Ingersol. "'With soap,'" Neva had said, "'baptism is a good thing.'" And she'd often recited a passage that went, "'Many people think they have religion when they are really troubled with dyspepsia.'" Every time she said this, Floris' teeth hurt.

Floris knew that Emory didn't care for the Ebenezers either, but he wasn't bitter about religion nor yet about life as was Neva. For instance, Floris knew he'd left for the lecture early in order to drive slow and see the sights.

Wherever he went, Emory took in the landscape. And watched the people who worked it. Although this was true, he sometimes looked with sadness now that the older farmers were dying off and the fields being covered with houses. As she'd watched Emory start off for Stafford, Floris had thought, *If I'd gone with him, I could have kept him cheerful.*

But she had business here to attend to. The book remained lost and there was this fool dog to be dealt with. He was still yapping just over the hill.

When Floris reached the cemetery, she got a surprise. One of the oak trees had come down during the night. Its roots had pulled out of the soil, and it had fallen across the raw earth of Neva's burial mound. What with the great trunk and all the twisted branches, a body could scarce make out where it was, exactly, that Neva lay.

Looking at the ruined tree, Floris felt a shiver go up her back. In bygone days, people had used to fell a tree across a grave on purpose to keep the spirits of the dead from getting out and pestering the living.

The old dog continued to bark. *It's a groundhog,* Floris guessed. *He's run it into its den and he's trying to dig it out.*

The earth up here was soggy from the storm. She felt a drip of rain on her arm. Stepping closer to the fallen tree, she peered down at it. The small leaves just starting on its branches were yet a fresh yellow-green. Where the bark was peeled back from the shattered trunk, the wood lay in white flakes like the flesh of a fish.

In the gray light of the afternoon, Floris glanced at the Sheridan grave markers. Some were thin limestone slabs, the inscriptions all but worn away by wind and rain. The more recent stones, of polished marble or granite, were thicker and more showy. Some had flowers or lambs carved on them. Or angels sitting at the top, shielding the stone with their wings.

"These folks are all in the hereafter," Floris whispered, "dancing with the Lord."

But Neva said, *Not me!*

The good, countered Floris, *go joyfully to God.* So, Preacher Doone of the Ebenezer Church said this. And the Bible said it.

"Everyone in Captina knows you were a good woman," Floris told Neva. "If you aren't in heaven, it's only your stubbornness to blame!" This was the whole point, of course. The point of needing to find *Elizabeth Drew.* Because there was no use whatever quoting a preacher or even the Bible to Neva. Scripture rolled off her like butter off hot corn.

But where Neva'd got no use for the Bible, she respected the British. She believed they'd got common sense. The Tones had come over from Yorkshire and they were level-headed as rocket scientists. So, Floris had counted on Elizabeth Drew to win this last argument between herself and Neva.

There's more to this world than our senses can fathom. So thought Floris. So wrote the authors Elizabeth Drew examined in her book. But before she'd read many pages, the book had gone.

"Oh, *where* has it got to?" Floris asked, and, her legs weakening, she sat down on the fallen oak.

Of a sudden, over the crest of the hill, here came Bugle racing down to her. He jumped about, whining and pawing at her knee, trying to enlist her help.

"Oh *hush!*" Floris told him. "I'm coming."

She got onto her feet and followed him up the slope, mortified that Bugle, dog though he was, had caught her talking to herself in a cemetery.

— 9 —

Emory

Just as Dr. Booker was about to, at long last, give them the low-down on *Viagra*, the lectern broke.

Emory missed seeing exactly what happened, but he judged the urologist had knocked against it with his elbow or his hand because the top part now hung a-slant, and the lecture notes once lying on it were winging out into the air and fluttering variously to the floor.

Any one of the men in the audience could have repaired the lectern. But Emory, having on his person both a screwdriver and packet of assorted screws, was the one who volunteered. During his later years he'd become well acquainted with odd jobs such as this. He was handyman to the village of Captina. He fixed broken things. Most of his work was done for helpless widow ladies like Mrs. Hopgood. He unstopped their toilets, greased their door hinges and joggled the soot from their chimneys.

He'd formed the habit of carrying tools about with him. Their weight in his pockets both defined him and joined him to the world.

While Emory sorted through his screws, Dr. B. and his secretary gathered up the spilled papers. Some of the men and women in the audience left the room for coffee or a smoke. The voices of those remaining made a low murmur that reminded Emory of bees.

On their honeymoon, he and Floris had come across a bee tree near the lip of the falls. They had watched, through the spray, the dark pellet-like bodies of the bees rising and circling. "Female bees," Flory had said to him, "are productive and industrious their lives long. When the males get old and useless, the ladies shove them out the door to freeze and starve."

She laughed and he laughed with her, not being old and useless then. Now, thinking back, he found himself less amused.

While Emory repaired the lectern, Dr. Booker said a few extemporaneous words about sex in America.

"Ours," he observed, "is a sex-centered nation. In our cinema, our music and TV, in politics, sports and business, a man is judged, not by his wisdom or his moral goodness, but by his virility. Especially if he's over 60. Indeed, about the time a man begins to be wise, off we shuttle him to a care center where like as not he sinks into profound, irretrievable silence."

Dr. Booker, Emory saw, now that he stood close to him, was himself approaching retirement age, which perhaps accounted for the urgency his voice had taken on.

"A whopping erection is our symbol of success," said the urologist. "So, we are fortunate to have methods, some lately devised, of enhancing flagging performance."

The doctor turned his back briefly in order unroll and pin up a large graphic of the male organ, its inner and outer parts labeled and delineated in differing colors. Wielding a pointer, he began a crisp, physiologically oriented, summing up.

As a lad, mused Emory, while tapping the tip of a screw into the lectern with the screwdriver's handle, he'd kept his member to himself. Later on, when he'd gone into the army, it had been necessary to wave it around in company somewhat.

But in his younger days he'd thought of his hidden asset with a sort of awe. On account, Emory supposed, of its as yet unknown possibilities.

Of course, for him, back then, the most mysterious, awesome spot in the universe was the private place of a woman. And the most exciting. And so beautiful when he'd come to know it at last that he'd felt, though he scarcely credited anything as being holy: *this comes close.*

Not much mystery left nowadays, was Emory's thought. Not much awe either. Wherever you looked, you saw private parts, both male and female, on display, either alone or interacting. They put him in mind of the illustrations in a book on pipe fittings.

His notions on the subject came, he supposed, from his being the product of a religious prude and a horse trainer. His mother had been a Methodist deaconess. Sex wasn't overtly mentioned at home, only hinted at as a dark and dangerous business linked some way or other with sin and disease. It was the horses that released him from guilt and fear into wonder.

He'd watched his dad attend a stallion covering a mare. It was an act of ardor and of violence. And of the most intense beauty. Afterward, Emory had often seen, in his mind's eye, mating horses. As he lay with Flory all through the years of his marriage, he'd seen them. There were nights he saw them still.

Not lately, of course. These spring nights since Neva's death he'd turned his face to the bedroom wall and let Flory read her book.

When the lectern was fastened back together, firm and trustworthy as Emory could make it, Dr. Booker thanked him and directed the audience to take a short break while he put his lecture notes back in order.

"Stretch your legs," said Dr. B. "Get your blood circulating. When we come back, we'll tackle *Viagra*."

— 10 —
Floris

Without shovel or pick, Floris couldn't give much help in digging out the groundhog. When Bugle's claws proved too broken and worn for the job, she coaxed the old dog back down the hill and, dragging him the last few yards across the garden, refastened him to his everlasting chain.

She kicked off her muddy shoes on the back stoop and entered the kitchen in sock feet. What she thought was this: *If the book wasn't in the restaurant or anywhere along the streets of Captina, then it must be somewhere in the house.*

Starting with the upstairs, Floris once again searched every room. Every closet. Every drawer and every shelf. She looked under and behind each piece of furniture. Beneath the edges of rugs. Amongst other books. In her sewing basket. Between the folds of blankets and towels. Behind soup cans and spice jars. Under Emory's pipe rack and inside the sheets of his newspapers. All the while she looked for the book, her mind dwelled on its image as if by so doing she might conjure up its actuality. It was an old book, well-worn. She pictured its faded spine. Its boards gone the soft, slatey color of shadow. The letters of its title, which, their lower parts rubbed away, resembled rows of rising moons.

The book's pages, brownish and pliable as old thumbs, were creased at the corners from being folded down. Thoughts and questions were scribbled in the margins. Passages were starred and checked. Underlinings were present, done in differing inks, various shades of graphite. Reading the book, Floris had felt in company.

And always she'd thought: *Somewhere in the world there are others like me. People who understand the world most clearly through words printed on a page.*

Stuck to the book's lower spine there'd been a white square marked with letters and numbers, which, for some reason, she remembered. Coda. PR 821/D7. And 1964, the year the library bought the book. Only the year had made sense to Floris.

Letters had also been stamped across the book's outside edge. When the pages were spread apart, the letters disappeared. When the book was closed, the words "Malaga College Library" appeared. The book was a puzzle and a mystery.

If, Floris speculated, *she had got through a chapter a night, she'd have finished the book long ago.* But as the practitioners of certain religions wore caps as protection (she believed) from the overpowering holiness of their God, she'd read only a few words at a time so as not to be overwhelmed by what she took to be the all but numinous ability of the book to set Neva's spirit free. Some evenings she hadn't opened the book at all but only held it in her hands.

At last Floris left off searching. Giving a sigh, she sank down in her rocker by the kitchen window. Out in the garden, Bugle was worrying at something. She couldn't make out what it was. She hoped he hadn't dug up the rabbit.

Setting her chair to a gentle rocking, she closed her eyes and of a sudden felt the book hovering before her, small and dark, like a floater in the eye.

As she'd read it, Floris had imagined Elizabeth Drew guiding her through a house where writers worked. Opening door after door, "This is Floris," said Elizabeth Drew. "Floris, this is Thomas Hardy. Emily Bronte. D. H. Lawrence, James Joyce, Virginia Woolf." The authors seemed to nod. A few reached out and shook her hand. She'd felt the warmth of their fingers on her palm.

Stuff! said a voice which was surely Neva's. *It was only a book and now it's gone. And,* said Neva, *I'm gone as well.*

And love-making's gone, or nearly so, thought Floris, imagining Emory at his lecture in Stafford.

Did God, she wondered, suffer loss? She thought of fallen angels and then of fallen men. What she suspected was this: *God never gives up on any of us.*

Floris stood and put on her slippers. Returning to her chair, she took the telephone onto her lap and, consulting the directory, punched in the number of the Malaga College Library. When a man's voice answered, she gave him her name, address and telephone number. Then she told him, "I'm sorry to say that I've lost one of your books."

"Our policy on lost books," he said, "is as follows: after a month's grace period, you pay the library forty dollars."

"Would the money," she asked him, "be used to replace the book?"

"This decision," he said, "would be left to the library board." The pang Floris suffered at hearing this was indescribable. It was as if she were responsible for a death. Duty-bound to replace *Elizabeth Drew* is what she felt.

After she'd hung up, Floris began calling bookstores. She tried the small one in Captina, the college bookstore in Robertsville and the two bookstores in Stafford. They all gave her the same answer. Elizabeth Drew's book on the novel was out of print. They had no copies on their shelves. They advised her to try second-hand booksellers.

She rang up a great many of these with no success. One second-hand dealer suggested she contact a book-searcher. "Look for their ads," he said, "on the back pages of the *New York Times Book Review*. And," he added, "in magazines."

Floris leafed through a stack of her gardening magazines and Emory's newspapers but found no ads for book-searchers. She sat for a while staring at the phone. Then she put on her sweater and knit hat and set off at a rapid pace toward the Captina Library.

— 11 —
Emory

Dr. Booker's talk was running longer than Emory had supposed. He thought he'd better ring up Floris and tell her to put supper back at least an hour.

In spite of the cookies, his stomach was commencing to register a vacuum. *What would Floris fix*, he wondered. *A chicken, it might be. And the elderberry pie.*

Emory liked to eat. Good food, of course, was another of life's delights. The foremost, he supposed, once sex was gone. He pictured the gold-brown crustiness of a chicken's roasted skin. Recalled the sour-sweet taste of elderberries bursting between tongue and palate.

Before he could ask where the telephones were, he had to wipe his mouth since it had commenced watering.

He approached an old fellow in a Rugby shirt with a mop of silver hair who said the phones were on the left just beyond the banquet room.

"I've had about all of that folding chair my sitter can take," said the man. "Besides which," he said, "my right leg's gone numb. I've got shrapnel in that hip from the Korean War. Were you in the service?" he asked Emory.

"I was," Emory answered, "but I didn't fight. I trained in Texas and served in Greenland."

"What'd they find for you to do up there?"

"I mostly enforced health regulations. Saw to it the food the army served the troops was fit to eat. Fish," Emory told the man. "Powdered milk. One hell of a lot of canned peaches."

"Well, I *was* in the fighting," the man said, his voice sounding somewhat weary. "Hamburger Hill. Other hills, too. We get together once a year, my old company. Those of us that're left."

Emory wondered, not for the first time, what his outlook on life would be if he'd personally killed other men, watched his buddies blown apart or witnessed, as some had in Vietnam, the slaughter of innocents. Or if he'd seen, as Neva saw, friends and lovers overdose as their ideals turned into carrion; seen a father poisoned by alcohol, a mother gone blind and, at the end, ravaged by cancer. *If I'd lived her life,* Emory asked himself, *would I be as much a nihilist as Neva was?*

Yet all of us, the Americans of my generation, thought Emory, *are war-ridden. We remember the second Great War and the little wars. Their evils hang in us like bats, and it takes very little to send them screeching and flapping about our brains.* Living through such times shriveled men's souls, Emory decided, whether or not they took part in the fighting.

And he wondered, not for the first time, why Floris, whose early life had been much the same as Neva's, was ever warmed by hope, while her sister, in her later years, existed in a despair colder than ever Greenland was.

Floris had tried to assuage Neva's frozenness with Reverend Hazzy's Pentecostal heat. Once or twice she'd even attempted to find her sister a beau. But nothing thawed her.

The truth was that Neva had had several lovers during her years of cross country travel. Guitar-players, some of them. Tree-huggers. Whale-fanciers. Social agitators. Acid-droppers. Mushroom-munchers. They'd been, each one, disappointing.

"Too many men," Neva'd once told Emory, "stay children their lives long. They chase after butterflies, while the world self-destructs."

He supposed she was speaking of the guitar-players. Or of her father.

In the late 1960s, Neva had ended her journeying to live on the west coast and work in a drug rehabilitation clinic. It wasn't until her father sickened that she came home for good. People said the Sheridan girls' dad lay on his deathbed singing songs of Ireland until the hour his breath stopped. And Floris sat beside him singing hymns. It might be, Emory speculated, that sharing a house with two such lotus-eaters was what set Neva's feet on the edge of the bottomless pit.

Of a sudden, Neva's flushed face, her restless black eyes rose before him, and he felt again the stab of sorrow he'd felt on the day she died. Sorrow for their loss, his and Floris'. Sadness for Neva because both living and dying had been so hard for her.

Before Emory had time to locate the telephones, Dr. Booker's secretary began blinking the lights to call them to the lecture room.

The gist of Dr. Booker's next remarks was this: although exceedingly promising, even the blue pill had its drawbacks. It could cause headaches, flushing, upset stomach and a bluish tint to vision. It could kill men with certain heart problems and possibly blind those with diseased eyes. And the pills were pricey.

As he'd promised, the doctor called for questions. At first no one put up a hand. Then a question was asked from the right side of the room, followed by one from the left. After the ice was broken, many hands went into the air.

Surprisingly, most of the questions weren't about impotence. They were about health insurance. The men wanted to know which amongst the described devices and treatments would be covered and which wouldn't. And, if they would, how much would be left for them to pay.

Dr. Booker appeared galvanized by these questions.

"For your health's sake," he told them, "you men shouldn't allow choice of treatment and medicines to be taken away from medical professionals and put in the hands of bureaucrats and businessmen. You should not only be able to pick a physician, but you should have input as to the procedures covered.

"Write to your insurance groups," he urged them. "Write to your government representatives. Write to newspapers and magazines. Let your needs and your opinions be known."

But most of the old fellows seemed to have a defeatist attitude. Of a sudden they were restless. Weary of the discussion. Ready to go home and, for the time being, forget about their impotence, both physical and political.

Dr. Booker took the hint. Gathering up his papers, he used them to wave good-bye.

With a scraping of chairs and a muttering of voices, the audience came slowly to its feet. When Emory stood, his knees hurt. And his lower back. He pulled on his cap and walked out of the lecture room, his joints slowly warming into smoother action. In the hall, he turned left toward the telephones.

— 12 —
Floris

Floris, stepping smartly across two blocks of cracked sidewalk, made a quick trip to the Captina Library. Marie Hale listened to her question about where to find book-searchers and offered help.

"We take the Tuesday *Times*. I'll check it and I'll check our magazines and let you know what I find," she said. "When are you coming back to work?"

Floris stared into Marie's round, earnest face, reluctantly meeting her inquiring eyes, magnified to the likeness of owl's eyes by her glasses. She felt herself pounced on.

"It's been nearly four months," said Marie. "We need you here, Linnet! Dorothy's doing an ant farm for the children. And then a puppet show. In two weeks, there's the book sale."

Floris hadn't considered going back. Couldn't bring herself to consider it now. She tried to tell Marie how, since Neva's passing, something inside her seemed to be hanging fire, seemed snagged and stopped and unfinished. Exactly what this was she found it impossible to explain to Marie or even to herself. Instead, she talked about needing to find the *Elizabeth Drew* book.

"I may," she finally admitted, "not be coming back at all. You should hire someone in my place." In truth she was surprised that this hadn't already been done. But Marie said 'no' and said it indignantly.

"It's you that Dorothy and I must have, Linnet," Marie told her. "You'd find yourself," she added, "the better for doing a little work."

Walking home, Floris remembered how, when her father died and, later on, her mother, Marie Hale and Dorothy Brinner came to the house. They'd been helpful and kind. 'The long and the short of it,' people called them because Marie stood near to five foot while Dot was well over six. Ever side by side, they went about Captina feeding the hungry, comforting mourners, nursing the sick, distributing books. And, of course, they gathered children together and read them stories.

Long ago the two old women had nicknamed Floris 'Linnet' after the small bird that feeds on blue flax flowers. Somehow she'd felt this gave them a strange power over her. It was as if, between them, they were the keepers of her secret bird soul.

She had enjoyed working with them. They were jolly women who loved to share a bit of harmless gossip and, now and again, a good off-color joke. Placid and benign, they often disagreed but always in a good-humored way.

Floris recalled the autumn day she'd come upon them raking leaves, the two elderly ladies in scuffed shoes and ragged jackets. While Dot held open a bag, Marie lifted in the leaves. As they labored, leaves, brown and gold, spiraled down on them from the branches above, brushing their shoulders, alighting in their whitening hair. One dropped onto the bridge of Dorothy's long, thin nose and balanced there a moment before descending to the ground at her feet.

"It's full," said Dot of the bag, but Marie stuffed in another armful.

"No more," Dot cautioned. "Tie it up quick."

"I can still squeeze in a few," said Marie and she did.

"You've put too many," Dorothy started to say, when all at once bang! the bag exploded like a bomb, sending a spume of leaves in all directions.

Marie, holding the rake, laughed. And Dot, holding the ripped bag, laughed. They laughed until tears ran from their eye-corners.

*

Returned home from downtown Captina, Floris lighted the oven. She fetched a package of elderberries from the freezer and placed it to thaw in a pan of warm water beside the sink. As she got out her rolling pin, what Floris thought was this: *Why was it that she and Neva could never laugh together at life's disasters in just such a way?*

— 13 —

Emory

Emory stopped at a water fountain and took several gulps. Listening was dry work. As he straightened, blotting his mustache on his sleeve, he saw his fellow-listeners pass by him and head out the double front doors of the Holiday Inn.

There went the dressy couple, his hand on her elbow. There went the man with the superlative hunting dog. And the veteran with his shrapnel. Last to depart were Doctor Booker and his secretary, wearing coats, she with a sheaf of papers and a box of slides, he lugging the projector. Watching them all disappear into the night, of a sudden Emory had the sensation that they'd all shared a bonding experience like a plane crash or being marooned on an island and he felt oddly bereft.

He cast one last look into the empty lecture room. On a bulletin board beside the door, someone had pinned up a notice concerning the next two lectures. The title of May's talk was "Prostate Cancer." June's was "Testicular Malignancy."

How will I die? When? Where? thought Emory, parroting Neva's habitual questions. Thinking of Neva, he chuckled briefly to himself, causing a woman disappearing down the hall to turn her head and stare back over her shoulder.

Neva's obituary called her death unexpected which tickled Emory since it was the one event which she'd been expecting all her life. In point of fact, Floris had found her in the garden, face-down in the snow. Her slippers were still on her feet and, about her knees, the skirt of her flannel nightdress flapped in the wind.

It was a stroke, their doctor told them, though why she'd run outdoors in such weather and at such an hour none of them could say.

"Sometimes there's an aura right before the stroke," the doctor said. "People hear a voice call their name or they're visited by some sort of vision." It might have been that, he said. Or it might not. "She may have just felt unwell and staggered about looking for help."

So they never knew what Neva's last thoughts were. Floris, as was her wont, entertained some fanciful religious notions of a conversion. But Emory, knowing Neva, supposed her last thoughts hadn't been too different from the thoughts she'd had her life long.

A small girl in corduroy overalls came scampering along the corridor bouncing like a beach ball. She resembled Floris and Emory's youngest daughter at that age and was just as impish by her look. She all but sideswiped Emory as she passed by.

Behind came her mama, frowning, her lips compressed. "Come back!" said the mama. "Come back!"

You may well say, "come back," thought Emory. *NOW she'll come back. In future, when you're my age and she is grown, she won't.*

Emory stood listening to the girl's laughter fade into the distance. "Nowadays the aged," Dr. Booker had said, "live out their lives shut away from the sounds of children."

As he walked on down the hall, Emory recalled how Floris was forever pestering him to take her visiting amongst their offspring while he, although wanting to go, yet hung back, loath to disrupt the children's busy lives.

— 14 —
Floris

From the cupboard Floris fetched shortening and flour. Lifted a pie pan off the shelf and set it ready. Inspected the oven and adjusted the heat and all the while the argument went on.

Neva, who had ever supposed them to be frauds, said this about the Ebenezers: "They feed you sop to ease your existential pain and to open your pocket-book."

Rev. Hazzy had entertained a low opinion of Neva as well. "Your sister," he'd often told Floris, "is stiff-necked." Sometimes, exasperated beyond endurance, he had gone so far as to call her demented. However, when in a better humor, he'd waxed hopeful and mailed her pamphlets and tracts.

As for Emory, Rev. Hazzy stuck labels on him, too. Puzzling over them, Floris had asked him to mark them down. Along the margin of her church program, he'd written the words 'prosaic' and 'hebetudinous'.

Floris carried the program home and showed the words to Emory. After looking them up in their *Webster's International,* they decided Emory stood accused of being an unimaginative bonehead.

The Ebenezers were Spartan of course. When she joined, Floris had to give up beads and ear-bobs. Nail polish and lip rouge. Dancing. And moving pictures depicting sex. Emory'd taken exception to all of it, especially the last.

"What've they got against nookie?" he wanted to know.

"Nothing," Floris assured him. "It's just if a body gets too fond of the pleasures of the flesh, they're like to numb the soul. Our Lord," Floris pointed out, "was celibate."

"How do you *know* he was?" asked Emory. "Did he *say* he was?"

Floris thought perhaps Paul said he was.

"Stuff!" said Emory, borrowing Neva's favorite expression. "How would Paul know? The two of them never even met."

Floris said they *did* meet. On the road to Damascus.

"Not in the flesh, they didn't," said Emory, "which," he begged to remind her, "is what we're talking here."

Remembering this exchange, Floris felt mortified. It was plain enough that Emory was a fool. And a blasphemer to boot. She nearly stopped making his pie. The kneading of the dough, however, soothed her. Also, the weather softened her toward him.

The oven had heated up the kitchen so that Floris opened a window and stood beside it breathing in the scent of moist soil and opening flowers. Springtime always brought back to her mind the first sight she'd had of Emory, a wild, dark-haired boy, lean and graceful, driving pacers around the track at the Bobtown fairgrounds, a morning mist curling about the sulky wheels.

Dashing, he was. And is, she thought, *with his white mustache and the white hair thick on his head.* Dreamily she rolled out the dough, lined the pan and poured in the elderberries, mixed now with sugar and flour. Admiring their deep purple color, she recalled the autumn day she picked them along the railroad tracks.

She remembered how she'd broken off stalks heavy with ripe berries and carried them down to the garden. There she'd sat gripping the blue enamel pan between her knees as she stripped off the tangy bitter-sweet fruit. The sun, come suddenly out from behind cloud, had touched her skin like warm hands. When she finished the job, her fingers were, every one, stained purple.

The Sheridans had used to make elderberry wine. They served it when they hosted the annual family reunion. On one such occasion, during her and Emory's courtship, Neva returned home, briefly, for the July get together.

Her sister got tipsy on the wine and, dancing with Emory to phonograph music out in the garden, she grabbed his John Henry. Everyone saw her do it. It was a scandal and an embarrassment to them all. Except to Neva who fell asleep shortly afterward and, upon waking, retained no memory of what happened. It became a secret joke between Emory and Floris down the years.

Just as she set the pie in the oven, Bugle commenced barking in the garden. Then a rapping sounded at the kitchen door.

When she opened it, there stood Marie Hale and Dottie Brinner just as they'd stood with their baskets of food when each of her parents died, and, then again, of course, when Neva passed. This time their hands were full of magazines and papers.

Floris threw wide the door, her arms still floury from pie-making. "Come in!" she cried, pleased to her soul by the sight of them.

"Here's enough book-searchers to keep you busy," said Marie, and they plopped their burdens down on the nearest chair.

"What a lovely smell!" cried Dot, sniffing round the oven door.

"Sit down," Floris had bid them. "I'll make coffee."

But they couldn't stay. They were on their way to present their case before the library board. The building was in dire need of a new roof.

"Did you hear the rain beat down last night?" Marie asked. "All that saved the Zane Greys from ruin was a plastic sheet I'd luckily draped over them to keep the dropping plaster off."

"Here's an item that'll make you laugh," Dorothy said, never one to leave without passing along a bit of tittle-tattle. "The Rev. Hazzy's Airedales got loose and overturned every trash can along Marple Street. When the reverend paid the fine, the mayor said to the dogs, 'Go forth and scrounge no more.' That was cheeky, wasn't it?"

The tall old woman and the short one stood side by side in Floris kitchen, helpless with laughter. And Floris laughed.

Stepping out the doorway, Marie said to Floris, "End your mourning, Linnet. 'Let the dead bury their dead.' Come back to work!"

— 15 —

Emory

Continuing down the left hallway in the Holiday Inn, Emory came, as the Korean War veteran had predicted, to a banquet room. Beyond it, at the hall's end, he found a pay phone.

When he heard Floris' voice on the other end of the telephone line, he felt, all at once, such an urgent need to see her that his knees went weak.

"The lecture ran on longer than they said," he told her. "But I'm starting home now."

"Do you want rice or potatoes with your chicken?" she asked him.

He said rice. "Did you find the book, Floris?"

"No." A sorrowful sound, this was. "Did you like the lecture?"

"Yes," he said, though from the way he said it, he knew she'd understand he hadn't liked it all that much.

The truth was Dr. Booker's remarks had struck him as not only vapid but useless. Because they'd never come again, those days of youthful passion, no matter what a fellow swallowed or injected or fastened on. Gone they were. Gone they'd stay. He hung up the phone, then jiggled the receiver, hoping his coins might, through some fluke, be returned. But they were gone as well.

Standing beside the phone, of a sudden Emory recalled their first kiss, his and Flory's. Her mouth, yielding and soft, had put him in mind of a handful of rose petals. It had given him the thrill of his life, that kiss. Remembering it, Emory almost picked up the phone and rang her again.

They'd been sitting together on a bench near the fairgrounds watching the moon climb up over the clock tower of Malaga College. She'd come to Bobtown with her dad to see the races. They'd become acquainted in the food tent, then taken a stroll about town while he told her with great exactness the proper way to curry a horse and how to look after its hooves.

The next day he'd gone with his father and the horses to another track in another county and after that another. And another. He hadn't got back to Robertsville for many a long day.

But when he did get back, he'd had no trouble tracing her to Captina. The Sheridans were well-known throughout the county. Evenings they'd sat on her front porch, smooching, until Neva, although she was the younger of the two, was sent out for a chaperone. Once, having walked him to the gate and closed it between them, Floris leaned her elbows on the top wire and said,

"When we kissed that first time in Robertsville, I saw an angel sitting on the clock tower."

He should have been warned then of the turns her mind might take. And yet he'd somehow understood it was their shared pleasure she meant. The surprising strength of it. The lifting and the soaring which neither of them had known was possible.

He'd understood this, Emory now suspected, because of his father. In some strange way his father's feelings for horses and Flory's angel were cut from the same cloth.

Afterward, during all his travels through the world, Emory never met another girl who claimed to see an angel when he kissed her. It was, he came to believe, what pulled him back to her at last, this assertion she made about their first kiss.

After the wedding, Emory stopped following the horses and moved into the Sheridan homestead with the two girls and their sightless mother. Too many women, he'd thought. And yet it had been a pleasant enough family group.

Their babies were born in that house and the four adults came to share a caring for these little ones and for one another almost deeper than hearts could bear.

Now the blind mother and the bitter sister-in-law were gone, the children grown and scattered, and he and Floris continued on in the old house on the remnant of what had once been the Sheridan Farm. He and Flory and Bugle.

Retracing his steps down the hall, Emory came to the banquet room. This time he stepped in and looked about the elegant, high-ceilinged chamber.

It was filled by long tables with chairs drawn up to them. Each table was covered with a white cloth and graced by a floral centerpiece. Plates were set out and silverware. To the right of each plate was a saucer under an inverted cup. Before the plates stood crystal goblets with white napkins stuffed into them, the edges fanning out like birds' wings.

Something about the hushed emptiness and the way the light from the hall shined in, picking out the rims of the plates and the stems of the goblets, caused words once read aloud by Rev. Hazzy to sound in Emory's ears: "I appoint unto you a kingdom as my Father hath appointed unto me. There you may eat and drink at my table in my kingdom."

Emory found himself unsettled by such an uncharacteristic recollection. As he backed out of the banquet room, he nearly upset a sign by the door. The sign read, "8 o'clock dinner meeting, Stafford Senior Citizens Association."

He walked past the sign and down the hall and pushed through the double doors. Soon he'd be home and he was glad of it. A man grew weary and craved his bed.

Had the lecture on impotence been worth hearing, the slides worth seeing? He honestly couldn't say. The possible cures seemed appallingly hazardous. Crossing the parking lot, he thought this about old age: *As it's holding the reins, a body'd do well to settle into the pace it sets.*

— 16 —
Floris

The pie sat cooling on the table. The chicken slowly browned in the oven with run-over juice from the elderberry pie bubbling beneath it.

Floris washed her hands and, seating herself once more by the telephone, took up the magazines and papers Marie and Dorothy had brought and began sorting through them, turning down the pages, marking those book-searchers she wished to try. After a while she got up and fetched the magnifying glass. She found the print uncommonly small.

Skipping over ads that said, "Out-of-print children's books," or "Rare books our specialty," or "Erotica," or "Collectors' first editions," she concentrated on the ones that said, "I can locate your book," "Free search," and "Experienced professional searcher will look vigorously for THE BOOK."

By the time Floris began to make her calls, it was so late in the day many of the numbers didn't answer or else she got recordings which she felt it beyond her to address.

At last a woman's voice came on the line. She identified herself as Josephine Adler. She was located in Camden, New Jersey.

An elderly woman by the sound of her voice, Floris thought. And she pictured her scurrying like a small grey mouse into musty second-hand book shops, spelling out faded titles on spines with quick, bright eyes behind wire-rimmed glasses. Though it was more likely she made use of a computer.

Hesitantly Floris said, "I want...I wish you to find a book for me."

Hearing this, Josephine Adler launched into a rapid, rather breathless spiel. "My business is finding out-of-print books. Give me the title, the author's name, the publisher and the year of publication, or as many of these as you are able, and I will begin a search. If you don't hear from me in three to four weeks, I did not find it." Ms. Adler's voice, detached, dispassionate, went on and on like a chant. Floris felt herself mesmerized. She thought of an undertaker discussing arrangements for a person she neither knew nor cared about.

"The charge for the book is not based on what the book cost when new or on the fact it is out of print but on supply, demand and condition. So much for paperback, so much for hardcover."

Floris gave Ms. Adler what information she had on Elizabeth Drew. She dictated her own name, address and her telephone number. As she hung up the phone, in spite of herself, Floris began to believe that Josephine Adler would indeed send her a copy of the lost book.

Once she held the book in her hands again she felt she could win this last argument with Neva. This argument that was wrenching her soul.

Thought Floris, *Here's what I'll do. I'll read out words written by, say, D. H. Lawrence or Virginia Woolf.* (Regretfully, she must leave out Joyce, an Irishman, and Conrad, a Pole.) The words of these writers weren't overtly religious and so wouldn't put Neva off. But listening to them she'd have to admit that caring between people was, as Floris believed, the gateway to God. Caring like the solid love there'd always been between Emory and Floris. Between the both of them and Neva herself.

These are BRITISH writers, Neva, she'd say, *every bit as level-headed as the Tones. And if they write, as some of them do, that there's more to life than our senses can reach, if they hint at some meeting on the other side of death, then you've got to admit it might be true!*

Promptly, Neva's voice spoke in her brain. *Worms are worms,* said Neva. *Rot is rot.* She didn't even bother quoting Ingersol back at her. If this was a battle of writers Floris had to admit Neva could find, in a multitude of books, references to a meaningless universe, a non-existent, absent or cruel God; views of the world that saw in human life merely ego and greed, hate and spite, and death as only a final oblivion. Like fencers she pictured them parrying, she and Neva, blocking, thrusting not with swords but with quoted words.

Were Neva to quote such negative writers, what could Floris and Elizabeth Drew offer that would convince her? Flora, being a truthful woman, had to answer, *Nothing much.*

Dusk had come and turned the window-glass into a mirror. In it, Floris saw herself sitting in her chair. Her small nose. Her white hair. When she leaned closer, she saw, through the pane, the empty flower bed below the window. And at once thought of the geraniums. Neva's geraniums stored downcellar since last fall. What with searching for the book and chasing after Bugle, she'd forgotten to bring them up to the light.

She went at once to seek them out. There they sat, four plants, each one in its separate pot. Dormant. Gnarled and ancient. Brown and stiff as old paper. Although Neva hadn't cared about most flowers, she'd liked geraniums for their spunk and hardiness. And for their brazen scent. Around them on the floor lay petals the color of dried blood fallen from last summers' blooms.

Floris brought the geraniums water. Once the roots were soaked, they sent up an odor strong as a shout. It spoke to Floris of Neva who had always done this chore. This watering. This moving of the plants out of the dark. Carrying the geraniums, two by two, up the cellar steps, she set them on the sill of the kitchen window facing south. When the sun touched them, they would unfurl green leaves.

"I don't want to bring you back," Floris told Neva, "into a life you found so bleak and hard to bear. I only want you to agree you'll move on into the Everlasting."

I'm better where I am, said Neva. *Leave me be.*

Opening the oven, Floris gave the chicken a poke with the two-tine fork. The elderberry juice, gone crisp and black, was on the point of subsiding into ash. With two spoons, she turned the chicken pieces. Setting pans of water on the stove to steam the broccoli and boil the rice, she judged the supper should be ready by the time Emory got home from Stafford.

"I'm hungry as new-born foal," Emory had told her before hanging up the phone at the Holiday Inn. "Get that chicken cooked!"

Floris had said she would.

— 17 —

Emory

The spring wind, redolent with the savor of awaken-ing plants, seemed of a sudden to quicken Emory's blood as well. He felt his member stir, he was certain this time, and he thought, *It's reaching toward the village. Or beyond it,* he surmised, *to where the Sheridan homestead stands on the west edge of Captina. It's reaching,* he thought, *toward Floris.*

He put an extra pressure on the gas pedal and the truck gave a moderate leap. Steadfast, it was, this truck, for all its gas-guzzling and advanced age. *A good trait in an automobile,* thought Emory. *And in a woman.*

Yet even as he had this benign thought, Emory felt an irritation with his wife that lingered and, like a tickle in the throat, grew stronger. Because of a sudden he felt this business with the book had gone on long enough. And this moping over Neva.

Emory told himself he understood why Floris found it hard to let her sister go. He pictured honeysuckle on a trellis.

Or a rose rambling on a fence. The honeysuckle and the rose were Flory. The trellis and the fence were Neva.

Yet in her own way, Emory thought, Floris was made of stouter stuff than ever Neva was. Where Neva said *no* to life, Floris said *yes*. Where Neva said *yes* to death, Floris said *no*. *Floris withstands*, Emory thought. *Floris endures.*

Emory was so sunk in his own thoughts, it was a long while before he heard the siren. A police car was close behind him, its lights flashing. He angled the truck over to the side of the road and turned off the motor.

Rolling down his window, he waited. Pretty shortly here came Billy Hale, nephew to Marie at the library. In his uniform with its badges and buckles, he looked even more unwieldy than he looked at the bowling alley where he and Emory rolled balls together on the Kanassat Hardware team. Billy'd grown big-stomached in his middle-age. So had Emory, somewhat. But Billy waddled as he walked.

Reaching the truck, he leaned over and peered in at the window. "You was going," Billy said, "a way too fast there, Emory."

"I'd got to thinking," Emory said, knowing this didn't count as much of an excuse. He'd been having conversations with people not in the car, a difficult thing to explain.

"Well, I got to write you a ticket, Emory." Billy pulled out his pad and steadied it against the hood of the truck while he filled in information. When he'd finished, he tore it off and handed the carbon copy to Emory through the window.

"I heard you and Lois finally got yourselves engaged," remarked Emory as he folded the ticket and stuck it into his shirt pocket. "When's the wedding?"

Billy flushed bright pink. "No time soon," he said.

"A man your age don't want to wait," Emory advised him. "Jump in there and use it, Billy," said Emory, "before you lose it."

"I tell you, 'slow down,' and you tell me 'speed up,'" remarked Billy. He ambled off toward his cruiser. "See you at the bowling alley," he said over his shoulder.

After Billy Hale drove away, Emory sat a while looking at the structure the truck's headlights were picking out of the dark. It was the Keystone Ebenezer Church.

The beams illuminated the blocks the church was made of, big chunks of orange-colored sandstone dug out of Wolf Pen Creek just down the hill. They were shaped by hand and fitted together without mortar.

On a glass-protected board set up in the front yard, Emory read the following, "Then Samuel took a stone and set it between Mizpeh and Shen, and called the name of it Ebenezer, saying, 'Hitherto hath the Lord helped us.' Samuel 7:12. Tuesday School, 9:30. Church, 11. Ahaziah Doone, pastor. 'Blessed be the name of the Lord.'"

Above the front door, another board bore the church's name. This name harked back to Bible times when Samuel was fighting the Philistines. Emory thought the Ebenezers seemed still to be fighting that battle. In their sermons and discussions, they referred to county residents who attended other churches, as well as to the unchurched, as 'Philistines.' Emory was one of the latter. He'd attended the Keystone Ebenezer Church several Tuesdays when Floris first started and every single time he'd felt out of place as a Parcheesi piece on a chess board. He didn't plan on going back anytime soon.

In truth what he'd itched to do was give Rev. Hazzy a dressing-down for getting his wife into such a stew over where her sister had got to. Fretting was she in heaven, in hell or just lying up there under the oaks on the hill. The uncertainty was making Flory's life a burden. And his life a burden as well.

Once he was home, he'd tell Floris as much. He would, in fact, make her a deal. *I'll stop fretting over sex if you'll give up on Neva and that fool book. Let's the two of us agree,* he'd say, *to grow old in peace.*

He turned the wheel and, giving the truck a spurt of gas, pulled back onto the road. Captina was just over the next little rise.

When at last Emory swung into the driveway of the Sheridan homestead, he saw Floris out in the garden. Bugle was with her and the two of them seemed to be flopping around like a couple of headless chickens.

— 18 —
Floris

When Floris glanced out the window, she saw Bugle in the garden and realized she'd forgotten to feed him. Her mind was like an open-ended poke tonight. Things slipped out of it and dropped away.

She fetched his dish, dipped dry food into it and added scraps she'd saved from the table. She ran hot water into the dish and set it on the floor to soak, smelling its fulsome gravy scent.

If nurturing had worth, she thought wistfully, then perhaps she, like Dot and Marie, had lived a life of service. Because all her days she'd fed the hungry. Pets. Farm animals, cows and sheep, pigs and chickens. Family. Hired hands. Distant kin and needful strangers. She'd set out good fare at Sheridan House even in the lean years. And always a crowd at table.

Gradually, though, the farm was sold off, this piece, then that piece. The animals were taken to market. The children grew up and departed. Friends and family dwindled. One by one they grew old, sickened and were gone. Now there was only Emory and Bugle to feed. Yet how they loved to eat, both dog and man!

She set bowls ready for the pie, a knife to cut it, a spatula to lift it out. She put their dinner plates, hers and Emory's, with the violets round the rims, at their places. Silverware. Saucers and plain white cups, since the ones matching the plates had, long ago, got their handles knocked off. Paper napkins. She made tea in the black pot with gold roses that Neva'd given them on their wedding day. "Though I suppose you'd as soon I had got you books!" Neva'd said.

"As to books," Floris said aloud to her sister, taking up an argument of former days, "Elizabeth Drew says books 'enhance and vitalize us. Writer and reader interact with one another,' she says, 'and with the society around them.'" Lacing the fingers of her two hands together, Floris held them up, triumphant.

Stuff! said Neva as Floris had known she would. *Reading is selfish because it's solitary. You might as well,* Neva told her, *be dead as forever sitting around with your nose a book!*

Dead as I am dead, Neva went on, her voice commencing to knoll like a bell. *No taste,* she said. *No smell. No touch. No sight, no sound, no movement, no thought. No heaven. No God. No love.*

"Just you wait," Floris said to Neva. "Just you wait!" Because of a sudden she'd remembered about the notes she'd taken.

She climbed the stairs and went into their bedroom, hers and Emory's, and switched on the lamp. One side of the bed, Emory's side, was against the wall. On the side toward the hall, her side, was a nightstand covered by a miscellany of both his and her belongings, all mixed together. Her hairbrush, his clippers. A jar of her face cream, his shoehorn. Several of her books, sports sections from his newspapers. Her nailfile, his dental floss.

Under the books she found her tablet. She scooted it out and turned over a page and another and another without finding the place where she'd copied out lines from *Elizabeth Drew.*

Time was running short. Very soon now, Emory would pull into the drive. Reluctantly she replaced the tablet on the nightstand. Back in the kitchen, sprinkling rice into boiling water, Floris watched the grains leap and dance. So joyful and abandoned they looked, she'd a yen to dance herself.

Of a sudden she remembered how her papa used to dance with her when she was small, she standing on his shoe-tops as he moved them both about the parlor floor in time to his whistling. And what she thought was, *why shouldn't she and Emory now and again dance to the juke box in Mindy's Homestyle Restaurant where they sometimes ate their suppers on a Saturday night? If the young people giggled, well, let them. If the Ebenezers were scandalized, so be it.*

Floris put a lid on the rice and turned down the burner under the kettle. When she judged the food in Bugle's dish to be softened enough for his old teeth to chew, she took it up, went out into the garden and set it down in front of him. He began at once to gobble it up.

As Floris was filling Bugle's water pan from the hose, she found, lying beside it, the split-bottom basket. He'd managed to pull it off the bench. When she lifted it to the light, she was surprised to find his teeth marks on the handle.

"You're too old a dog for puppyish chewing such as this," is what she told him.

Placing the basket back on the bench, she saw that he had torn out the bottom as well. Bits of basket were scattered over the garden. Lighter-colored than the grass, they looked like dead moths. Or like the severed wings of birds.

While the old dog ate, Floris stepped into the side yard and, gathering several daffodils, laid them on the stoop. She wanted a bouquet for the table.

The blooms, some yellow, some white, were closed because of the cold. After she got them inside and stuck them in water, they would begin slowly, slowly to spread their petals.

The flowers made Floris think of certain people she knew. Of neat, shy, well-regulated souls like Marie and Dorothy who kept their lives well-ordered and their feelings to themselves. They reminded her of herself.

Emory's mother had been a different sort of person. Upright and spiky. More like a gladiola. Never a hint of powder or rouge. A braid of ginger hair tight pinned over her ears. A strait-laced, somewhat joyless disciplinarian, she'd lived her life according to the strict mandates of her church. *Which, like as not*, mused Floris, *is why Emory mistrusts the Ebenezers*.

"The only time I saw her unbend," Emory had said, "was when my dad came leaping into the house and swept her up in his arms. Her little feet would leave the floor and she'd laugh out like a child."

Sexually, thought Floris, some women were like Snow White in her glass box. They needed to be jarred awake. She herself had had no notion of sex until Emory's touch made her blood burn. She believed that, with boys, such first feelings came earlier and in a different way. Came, it might be, when they were riding a horse or shinnying up a tree. One day they felt it. One day there it was. And it was *with* them, insistent and momentous, for the rest of their lives. *Even when the ability to perform the act is gone*, mused Floris, *the memory stays to tell them who they were*.

For a woman, Florence suspected, sex was more complex. To begin with, it was part of the mating process along with romance and fanciful sentiments. Later it was an element of nesting, childbearing, and nurturing. A fragment of this whole. A thread woven through this larger pattern. Important but not all-important. *With sex, I'm Floris*, she said to herself. *Without it, I'm Floris still*.

After Bugle had cleaned out his dish, he began cavorting about her, trying to get hold of the ruined basket which she now held high above his head.

"Bugle, what possesses you?" Floris said to him. "You've gone back to your early days!"

And was just commencing to gather up the chewed fragments from the ground when headlights swept into the drive, and she saw that here was Emory come home at last.

—19—
Emory and Floris

They went into the kitchen together, she with her hands full of the destroyed split-bottom basket, he carrying a sheaf of Dr. Booker's hand-outs.

As she told him about her fruitless search for her *Elizabeth Drew*, Floris sensed he was irked by her obsession with the book while Emory, recounting the gist of the lecture, understood she found the ideas put forth by Dr. Booker not only boring but ridiculous.

By this time it was long hours past their usual meal time. They were, both of them, hungry and cross.

While Emory went to visit Bugle, Floris lifted the broccoli from the refrigerator. She carried it to the sink, ran water over it and searched it for green worms. She stripped away the leaves and sliced off the woody ends.

Two nice dark green heads. Expensive, Floris thought, but Emory liked broccoli, especially out of season. She'd bought these as a treat.

She laid them in the steamer, at the same time lowering the burner under the rice kettle to let it finish cooking at a slower pace. She looked in at the chicken and switched the oven down to 'warm.'

He's jealous of that book, she thought. The words came into her mind like a revelation. She pressed her lips together and raised her chin with an affronted expression.

When he sat down on the garden bench, Bugle came pushing his grizzled head onto Emory's knees. As if he'd say, thought Emory, *Remember all the coons we treed together?*

Emory stroked the old dog's ears reflecting that hunting in the woods or exercising pacers at the track, he'd felt comfortable, while here, sitting on this bench, he felt ill at ease.

Perhaps because this was where Neva had plaited her rugs and where Floris read her books.

He fancied Flory's bookish ponderings were pressing round him and Neva's nihilistic ones. He found himself in tune with neither.

It seemed to Emory that Flory's notions were paper-thin and insubstantial as the pages of the books she got them from. And while he and Neva had, together, ridiculed the Ebenezers, and though his belief in a personal God was gone from him, he found that his spirit yet suffered from a sense of answerability to some intuited Presence. Most probably his mother was to blame. But there it was.

Emory felt he stood at a parting of the ways from both the sisters. Except for old Bugle, he felt pretty much alone. He felt old. And defeated. Beside which he was god-awful hungry!

He speculated concerning his supper: was it ready yet? Emory stood up and Bugle, dispossessed of lap, nosed about under a forsythia bush beside the bench and came back with something in his mouth.

Another piece of the split-bottom basket, Emory supposed, but when he felt it, he thought it wasn't that. It was some other thing Bugle had been chewing on. Emory took it away from the dog and, having touched its edges, understood that it was Flory's book.

He carried it carefully, using both his hands, into the kitchen. When she saw it, she sucked in her breath with a sharp sound.

She took it from him and cradled it, he thought, as one would clasp a dead child. Holding it thus, she began to weep.

Which was too much for Emory. "It's only a book," he said. And at once wished he'd bitten his tongue instead. The glare she gave him took his breath away.

"He tore it up," wept Floris, "just like he did to the basket!"

"You'd tear up books and baskets, too," said Emory, "if you spent your life at the end of a chain."

"In a manner of speaking," she said, "I do."

What did she mean by that? he wondered. It was one of those wounding speeches women make to men, enigmatic and vaguely accusing. And she hadn't fetched in his newspaper, although by her own word, she'd got energy enough to traipse all over Captina looking for the fool book.

"Neva wove that basket," Floris said.

Emory, although he didn't say so, found he was sick to his soul of hearing about the basket and the book. And about Neva.

"What you can't help," he said, "you'd best put up with. The book," he pointed out, "was most likely ruined even before the dog chewed it. It laid out in last night's storm."

What Floris thought was this: *Before ever I began to search for it, the book was a book no longer.* She thought, *God knew this and let me go on searching.* And she felt betrayed and overcome with bootless grief.

Emory went out and down the drive and came back with his paper. Instead of unrolling it and glancing at the headlines as he always did, he threw it with a loud slap under the table. Floris jumped. Feeling enfeebled, she laid the book, its binding cold and slimy under her fingers, the pages mashed and sodden, down on a chair. The blood beat in her skull like a hammer.

"Well, it appears," Emory pronounced, "that all your searching was what they call 'an exercise in futility.'" He said this in a nasty-sounding voice. And although it was what she had just finished thinking, it raised her hackles.

"You can't fathom," she informed him coldly, "what that book meant to me."

Now *he* saw red. "I'm too hen-headed to understand, is that it? Not deep like you?"

"If the shoe fits," she agreed. "Every time I try to share my thoughts with you, you don't listen. All you care for is your stomach," she said, "and your John Henry."

He resented this mightily.

"Floris," he said, "you are so goddamned bookish you'd bore a saint."

With her face drained of color and her hair standing on end, she resembled an angry cockatoo.

"The last Sheridan reunion," said Floris, "you *gorged* yourself on Cousin Gert's current tarts. I was ashamed!" Her face now had more than enough color.

"I eat," Emory admitted. "And occasionally, I fuck," he said, "but not in my imagination. In the real world. A place," he told her, "you're scarcely acquainted with."

As he spoke, she watched his arms swing up and down in the air. He seemed about to beat the chair holding the book's remains into the floor with his fists.

"I *am* acquainted with it!" she said.

"You," insisted Emory, tapping her chest, "don't live in Captina. You live in cloud-cuckoo land." He kept poking at her with his finger until Floris had a great urge to close her teeth on the end of it.

"This supper's real enough," snapped Floris. "I've been holding this supper for you forever. It's taken," she said, "hours out of my life."

But he was lost in his own eloquence. Floris had heard men talking as he was talking before. On soap boxes in parks.

"You *live* in your goddamned books," he said. "You see the people around you as characters of your own fancy. That's why," he told her, "the children moved so far from home. So they can be actual and not as you imagine them.

"You never," he pointed out, "knew Neva. You made her up."

This stung. "No!" said Floris.

"Look how you dressed her in her casket," urged Emory. "If she gets up out of her grave as you're wanting her to do," he said, "she'll die again of mortification when she sees what she's got on. She always hated that polka dot dress."

Floris stood there wishing to call him by the words Rev. Hazzy had applied to him but unable to get her tongue around either one of them.

"Well, I know the real *you*," she told him scathingly, "if I don't know another living soul."

But he said, "You don't. You've never seen me as I am. You see me as some marble-assed hero in a book! Even in bed," said Emory, "it isn't me you're doing it with. It's Heathcliff. Or it's Lord Jim. Or it's that old bastard Rochester!"

Floris stamped her foot. "*You* don't believe in anything you can't see or hear or lay hold of," she said. "Neither did Neva. Old Bugle's better than the both of you. He's nearly blind and deaf, he's all but lost his sense of smell, but in springtime he knows when the rabbits come round him. This very afternoon, he caught one! He felt it with his soul. Y*our* soul," said Floris, "is a tiny, shriveled thing like a moldy prune."

Emory felt she needn't have said "moldy." His breathing hurt him. For some reason, his ears commenced to ring.

"Bugle caught a rabbit?"

"I buried it amongst the tulips."

"That's why he's taken to chewing things," said Emory. "Spring's put him in a hunting mood and that's made him feel he's young again."

Emory thought he'd like to see this rabbit with his own eyes. How many years had the old dog lived, made useless by his age-related infirmities, and never tasted rabbit fur nor rabbit blood, he who lived for that alone?

Out the door Emory went, more interested in a dead bunny, Floris noted, than in any understanding they might come to. She looked about her, feeling dazed.

She took the pan from the oven. The chicken had dried up. It was hard to the touch. The rice stuck together in a glutinous ball. The broccoli had boiled dry. The kettle and the steamer were blackened. The broccoli itself was mush.

Floris found that her stomach was clenched tight against her backbone. No use in sending food down there! It would just come back up, even if it wasn't burnt and spoiled. *I'll go to bed*, she thought. *I'll go to sleep. Tomorrow must be a better day.*

She lingered on a while gazing at the book. Like the broccoli, it was mush. With an effort she opened her fagged and listless brain and let it go. Let it depart from her, along with the need to hold it in her hand and to read aloud to Neva from its pages.

This was the moment when Floris understood she must very soon let Neva go as well. A harder task by half. This time it was her heart she must pry open. After thinking these thoughts, she could scarcely climb the stairs, her knees had gone so weak.

Emory set Bugle free of his chain and together they found the rabbit where Floris had buried it. He let the old dog grub it up and lick the fur while he whispered a word or two of praise into his ears. Then Emory dug a deeper hole, laid the rabbit in it and covered it over.

When he returned to the kitchen, he heard Floris moving about their bedroom overhead. He lifted the book from the chair and, carrying it back out to the garden, buried it on top of the rabbit.

Afterward he removed his big, muddy shoes and set them beside Floris's muddy little ones on the stoop.

Back in the kitchen, he glanced at the food sitting on top of the stove where Floris had left it. And found he had no craving to take any of it into his mouth. Switching off the lights, he followed Floris up the stairs.

She was in the bathroom. He shed his clothing helter-skelter onto the bedroom floor, pulled his nightshirt over his head and climbed into bed, feeling wretched and unwell. And cold, especially his extremities.

He lay back against the bolster waiting, as one does with roiled water, for his mind to settle. This is what he thought: *It's easier to buy baubles for a woman than to satisfy her thirst for weighty conversation.* And he wished Floris was one of the vain and greedy, feather-headed sort. But wished it only briefly.

All my life, Emory reflected ruefully, *I've stood on a battleground between two warring, strong-willed women, Floris and her sister. They were indeed their parents' children,* he told himself, recalling the blind mother and the drunken father. Which was an unkind thought and he was ashamed of it.

Down the years, although Emory's thinking had tended towards Neva's negative outlook, he'd never brought himself to side with her. Once she'd said of God, "If there *is* one, He's either a bungler or boar-hog mean." Emory opted for a third choice, that of prankster. Because he had to admit what drove him crazy about Floris was exactly what he loved in her the most. *On our wedding day,* Emory thought, *God had a good laugh.*

Of a sudden in his mind's eye Emory saw Floris as she was early each June kneeling in their garden, planting exotic seeds. Like so many things she did, she ordered them believing the impossible: that they would grow and flourish in Captina. And, although he couldn't believe in the impossible himself, still, watching Floris believe in it was more of a treat than anything else in his life. Except, perhaps, for bowling a 300 game. And, on this thought, Emory began to snore.

When Floris came out of the bathroom, she rummaged among the items on the nightstand looking for her face cream. The noise brought Emory back awake. He climbed out of the bed to take his turn in the bathroom.

Spreading on the cream, Floris made note of new wrinkles and, brushing her hair, marked its thinning. Replacing the brush on the stand, she discovered the tablet she'd left there. She looked through it again and this time found the jottings she'd made while reading *Elizabeth Drew*. She hadn't read straight through the book, saving that for later, but had sampled here and sampled there, finding treasures.

When Emory returned, wiping toothpaste from his mustache, he found Floris sitting on the side of the bed with the tablet in her hand. He crawled past her and arranged himself for sleep, pulling the covers up to his chin. Floris, as he had suspected she might, commenced reading aloud.

"Virginia Woolf," Floris declaimed, "'found, behind and within everyday things, a mystic affirmation of reality.'"

Emory more or less covered his head with the quilt.

"James Joyce," she continued, "'presented the artist escaping from bondage. 'A masterpiece,'" here Floris's voice rose with the excitement of rediscovery, "'isn't the absence of faults. It's the presence of a compelling creative intelligence'!"

She looked over to Emory, expecting a comment but he was asleep. Neva, as it turned out, was the one who commented, although her observation was more upon herself than upon the reading. *I am nothing*, Neva's voice said in Floris' ear, *but cold meat*. Floris had a brief memory-flash of Neva lying in her casket, her lips strangely pursed as if, in death, she spat on the Unknown.

However, Floris refused to be drawn into the old argument. She had begun to feel better about the destroyed book. Surely she would see *Elizabeth Drew* again. Perhaps the book-finder would succeed in her quest. One day she would have, not the poor ruined tome, but another copy. *And*, she thought, with a dart of excitement, *there are other books*.

Emory woke for the second time to find his wife energetically drawing on her rose-colored woolen robe.

"I'm going to have a piece of that pie," she said. "You want some, Emory?"

He did. They went down the stairs together.

At the kitchen table they sat in their accustomed places, amicably passing back and forth the milk pitcher and the sugar basin. They always ate their pie Yankee-style, in a bowl with milk on it.

When they returned upstairs, Floris found, gathering up Emory's discarded clothes, that one of his socks had a large hole at the toe. "Look at that!" she said.

She got the clippers from the nightstand and trimmed his toenails for him, careful not to nick the skin nor cut too close to the quick, careful to make them smooth and straight across.

As always, this took some doing. Emory's toenails were hard as metal. Each time she snipped, the paring leaped into the air like a grasshopper. Watching this, Emory and Floris giggled.

Flory's laugh, as it ever did, lifted Emory's spirits, making him feel illogically hopeful so that, when they'd got back into bed, he speculated that after all he might as well pick the one of Dr. Booker's cures likely to do him the least harm and give it a try. Keep on keeping on for a while longer. Having made this resolve, for the third time Emory fell asleep.

Floris napped and woke, napped and woke as old people do. Once, waking, she decided it was time she went back to work at the Captina Library. She could begin by sorting out volumes for the book sale, then clear off a shelf in the children's room for the ant farm.

She dozed for a time, then, opening her eyes, remembered tomorrow was Emory's bowling night. She'd need to fix an early supper. *Haddock*, she thought. *With baked potatoes. Emory liked a baked potato now and again. Split open and butter melted in. A little pepper. A little salt.*

When Emory got up to pee at 3 A.M., he woke Floris by climbing over her feet, and she sat up and told him her dream. She stood beside the Niagara River, she said, just above the falls, watching the limb of a white oak tree spinning in the current.

How it leaped! How it plunged and twisted! It seemed to be fighting with the rapids, trying to tear itself free. But, related Floris, the river carried it along whether it would or no until it hung on the very lip of the falls.

There it stopped, wedged between two rocks while, under it, the river thundered over the precipice.

In her dream it had seemed to Floris the branch teetered on the edge of the great declivity until at last, tugged by the might of the river's running, it fell into the dizzying downrush and, enveloped by spray, plummeted from sight.

Running to the edge, Floris told, she'd been in time to see it reappear at the foot of the falls, and to watch it float away through the gorge on the calmer waters far below. Floris commented that she believed her dream had somehow to do with Neva.

As it happened, Emory had also dreamed. In Emory's dream one of Rev. Hazzy's children tried to flush a deflated soccer ball down the parsonage john. Emory had spent a large part of the night trying, without much success, to unstop it.

What Emory thought was this: *Their next pieces of elderberry pie should be eaten earlier in the day.*

As she was awake, Floris took another turn in the bathroom. Emory raised the bedroom window an inch and stood for a time looking down into the garden. Starlight was reflected from the flat surface of the bench. In front of it, Bugle's lank chain sparkled in the grass. As night air aggravated his rheumatism, the old dog slept in the kitchen on Neva's unfinished rug.

Switching off the light, Emory crawled into bed. Husband and wife re-settled themselves, each on their accustomed side. When, just before falling asleep, Floris reached over and gave Emory's member a pat, it stirred somewhat, wishing her goodnight.

Tuesday at the Airport

Addie removed her new glasses with the distinct feeling that the lens prescription had somehow gone wrong. They gave her trouble reading and sewing. And now, in making out the faces of people at a distance. She was the more annoyed since these people, clumped about TV sets, seemed to be talking excitedly.

Something's happened, she thought. *But what?*

Too far off to hear, too distant to see, communication with her fellowman all but broken off, she felt herself slip, of a sudden, into a mild state of panic. She replaced her glasses and peered through them about the air terminal, seeing little.

The day of her optical examination, she had tilted her head against the back of the chair while the doctor put drops in her eyes. These had felt cold and made a bitter taste at the back of her throat.

"Look past me," said the doctor. His voice had a soft, coaxing tone. "Look up and to the right," he said.

When she looked, she saw colors. A bright light. What she saw was a fish. Or like a fish. Far off. Iridescent. It was her eyelashes, perhaps. Or rainbows from the bright beam of the eye-doctor's electric torch. This fish-like image appeared to look back at her, appeared, moreover, about to speak.

Then suddenly, instead of a fish, she saw the doctor's face. It thrust suddenly into her line of vision. She saw his cheek. The pores on his left nostril.

"A cataract is coming," the doctor said.

He made a note in his book.

Later, fitting her for frames, the technician laid a hand along Addie's cheek saying, "Move closer." Addie leaned and the technician leaned. They leaned toward one another.

No one's touched me since Mama died, Addie'd thought, and she'd had, all at once, a jarred feeling as if some heavy thing had fallen from her ribcage down into her stomach.

"What is it that's happened?" Addie asked of a woman who was passing, pulling a suitcase-on-wheels.

"It's the space shot," the woman said. "They just showed pictures of the astronauts," said the woman. "They were waving."

*

Early this morning while packing her lunch, Addie had switched on the radio and caught news about the impending space launch. There was concern over the bitter weather. And they had talked about the schoolteacher who was to be on board.

Addie thought of her mother, who had once been a teacher. If given the chance, Mama would have gone into space. No doubt about it. Her life long, Mama'd had a white-hot curiosity about everything in this world and the next. It was as if she were forever running a fever.

"What, exactly, is the point?" Mama used to ask. She meant the point of life. Of creation in general and of man's existence in particular. She put this question to everyone but most insistently to Addie.

*

By the time Addie got herself up and over to the nearest TV set, she found a soap opera playing. A woman was sobbing while a man shouted at her. Such trumpery set Addie's teeth on edge, especially as it wasn't real.

She passed through the sliding glass doors that opened so strangely of themselves, like walls in the mind melting away, she thought, and stood examining the headlines of the morning newspapers displayed on racks in the vestibule.

"Ah! This happened" they shouted in large black print. "Oh! That happened!" And most of it was perfectly horrid. Murders. Rapes. Robberies. All of which, quite naturally, attracted people's interest. *How awful!* they thought. *But it isn't me.* And they bought a paper.

This morning, however, every front page was given over to the nearing space launch. There were photos of the astronauts grinning and waving. Every one of them seemed eager to go.

Not for me, Addie thought. *No.* She'd not like being shot up high into the air where she'd be cut off from the rest of the world. Except for a two-way radio which, mused Addie, might malfunction and then where would you be?

*

"Keep your luggage and personal belongings with you at all times," boomed a deep, bodiless voice. The first time she'd heard the voice, Addie'd thought, *That's God speaking!* However, it was only airport security.

Suppose you set your valise down and walked off. Right away, airport security thought, "She's got a bomb in there!" And out they came, blowing their sirens, and snapped their cuffs on you, meanwhile squirting foam on your valise. Addie had never seen this happen, but she knew it sometimes did.

Besides God, the voice put her in mind of Mama. Of Mama's voice the way it had used to blare through the rooms of the house on Valhalla Drive. Of course, airport security's voice was a bass drone where Mama's had been more of a soprano shriek. And, of course, Mama didn't mention luggage. She asked her usual question. "Oh, WHAT," Mama would bleat, "is the POINT?"

As with airport security, you couldn't prepare yourself. You never knew when she was going to erupt. Sometimes she'd be sitting in the laundry room sprinkling clothes. Or standing at the stove frazzling onions. Or leaning forward on her bed knotting up her hair. At the least likely times, the need would come on Mama to ask her question. All down the years, Addie'd felt guilt-ridden because she couldn't answer it.

This was the same over-active sense of guilt that made her quake when airport security spoke. For the briefest of moments, she felt she *did* have a bomb in her valise, while in reality what she had was a peanut butter sandwich and a Granny Smith apple.

The valise, old-fashioned but not at all worn, was Mama's. It had purple embroidery on the sides and a clasp like a coin purse at the top, under leather handles.

Mama'd used it only once. She'd carried it on her and Papa's wedding trip to Mussel Shoals. The trip was a disappointment to Mama. The mussels, she said, were mighty hard for people to make out, peering at them as they must through rippling water. She was disappointed in other ways, too. Yet she'd always kept her fondness for the valise.

Addie carried it to make herself inconspicuous. Her desire was to watch and listen to the people around her while remaining unnoticed. In this way she hoped to prepare herself for the day of reckoning.

Because, ever since Mama died at the age of eighty, Addie had nursed the unshakable notion that, when *her* turn came to climb the golden stair, she'd find her mother standing at the top.

"Well," Mama would cry out, "what WAS the point of life, Addie Mae?"

By then, of course Mama would know. But she'd want to hear the conclusion Addie had reached on her own.

So far, the pure truth seemed to be that life *had* no point. At least none to speak of. Because what Addie heard most people saying, although not in so many words, was this: "*I* am the point of life. Look no further," they said. "It's *me!*" Hearing this, Addie turned hopeless. She felt like giving up the quest. But she never did.

*

Now, as it had gone ten A.M., Addie told herself it was time to stir about. Time to find a good spot in the midst of the crowd and perk up her ears.

The room where tickets were confirmed and boarding passes issued was narrow and long and high-ceilinged. It was full of noise and movement as a medieval hall. Addie went and stood in the ticket line for USAir. She set her valise down beside her and, as the line advanced, pushed it forward with her foot. With each shove, inside the valise, the sandwich and apple shifted, then came once more to rest.

In front of Addie two young men spoke of an approaching soccer game. They favored opposite sides. The more they talked, the crosser they became until each declared his hope of seeing the other team, along with all of its fans, removed to the nether regions. At the rear of the line, three women tattered about an adulterous office romance.

When Addie neared the ticket desk, she left USAir and joined the queue for TWA where a girl with a backpack played radio music into her ears through headphones. Eyes blank, she jiggled to its secret rhythm. *She's more removed from the world*, thought Addie, *than the astronauts would be on their space flight*. Nearby, a man and a woman discussed the ethnic cleansing aspect of certain foreign wars. After TWA, Addie tried the line for Delta.

When her corns commenced to hurt, she left the ticket lines and walked down the long echoing corridor to the metal detector and, her sandwich and apple having passed successfully through the machine, entered the area filled with airline patrons waiting for their flights to be called. She found herself a seat in a row of red plastic chairs where, her valise on her lap, she watched the people pass to and fro.

"Wait up a minute," said an elderly woman with a blue rinse on her hair. She sat down across from Addie and began to scrabble in the pockets of her coat. Her companions, a tall, thin woman and a man in a farmer hat, dropped into chairs on either side of her. "I can't find my car keys," the blued woman said. "Every day," she said, "I lose track of something or other." She opened her purse and poked through its compartments taking out, first a hankie, then a nail file, then a package of Dentine gum.

"Have a chew, Rhonda," she said. "Have a chew, Charlie." She helped herself to a stick, meanwhile lifting up a thin wallet. "I don't carry much money," she said. "I'm afraid I'll misplace it."

"When Montgomery had his stroke," said Rhonda, "he was carrying over four hundred dollars."

And now Charlie spoke up. "I carry about that," he said.

"Why do you men do that?" asked Blued.

Charlie shrugged. "Just don't want to be caught without it, I guess."

"Somebody at the Pick n Pay might see it," pointed out the tall woman. "Might foller you out into the parking lot."

"My sister had her purse stole from her church pew," observed Blued. "People don't care what they do anymore."

"I never carry it where I carry my grocery money," said the man.

Blued found her car keys under a clump of Kleenex and the three of them got up and moved on.

*

Often at night, alone in the house on Valhalla Drive she'd once shared with her parents, Addie lay awake listening for a robber to break in the back door. She slept in the bed where her father had died of a coronary infarction at the age of seventy-five. His death had left a rent in Addie's life through which cold winds of apprehension blew on her. When she was small and Papa vigorous and young, she'd felt no harm could befall her. None.

Papa was as close as she'd ever come to having a beau. Except, perhaps, for one other. When she was a girl, he had treated her with courtly reserve. Bowed to her. Pulled out her chair. Called her, "Miss Addie," or, sometimes, "Sweet Adeline." He'd said over the words of the old song to her. "You're the flower of my heart," Papa'd said.

For employment, Papa had sorted mail while riding on a train. She'd always pictured him, head bent, fingers full of messages, sealed and secret unto themselves, traveling swiftly through the night.

He was an undemanding man. Just as he never opened the letters he sorted, so he never tried to break the seal of her private thoughts.

He spent his free time on a small plot of earth behind the house where he watched birds and cultivated vegetables and flowers, meanwhile making, among his tenderest feelings, a place for *her* to grow. If he changed somewhat down the years, Addie kept his earlier image present in her mind.

The day Papa died, Addie thought she dropped down a well. Seeing him lie cold and still, she felt ice begin to float in her blood. When she touched his hands, they seemed changed into outcroppings of rock.

*

Addie had watched Mama and Papa grow old. Now she was old herself. Bent over, somewhat. Not so heavy nor yet so tall as she once was. White-haired and dewlapped, she became, day by day, increasingly mistrustful of her balance. And of her ability to cope with the world.

Sitting in the airport chair, she looked down at her fingers, grown big-knuckled from arthritis, and thought, *Our hearing wanes, our sight dims, our touch grows painful so as to wean us away from the world. To make it easier for us to leave it. Our physical selves fade while our spirits wax louder like radio stations changing places late at night. In old age,* she thought, *as we reach out to others, we begin to touch not their bodies nor their minds but their souls.* Whether these notions were true or untrue she couldn't say.

*

A freckle-faced boy flopped down beside her. He was eating a hot dog. Across the way, a young woman in a linen suit read a book. She turned the pages slowly, now and then under-lining a passage with a yellow marker. Addie craned her neck, trying to discover the title.

Addie herself had spent the better part of her days reading books. Volumes on the religions of the world. Philosophy. Physics. Psychology. Sociology. Astrology and phrenology. By and large she'd found them unhelpful in framing an answer to her mother's question. The knowledge they contained breezed in and out of her brain leaving behind only a puzzling rubble like the deserted nests of birds.

Nor had she, in her younger days, found work anymore enlightening than books. Most of her life she'd had selling jobs. She'd sold now this, now that. Clothes. Baked goods. Pet supplies. Potted plants. She'd not been so much interested in the wares nor the selling as in the salary which let her buy things for Mama and for Papa.

Her parents had been her world. The three of them, Mama, Papa and Addie were a universe unto themselves. They were uncommonly close. They'd come up to Tapp City out of the Appalachians, leaving kinfolk and friends behind. Their memories and their caring were rooted in another place. All they had left to them of that place was one another. Which might explain, somewhat, Addie supposed, why Mama had agonized over life's significance.

The patterns, the rhythms Mama had once known, the activities that gave her life its form and significance, were lost back among the hills and hollows of Colerain County. Where she'd used to anchor her life in harvest festivals and quilting bees, in animated talk at wedding ceremonies, christenings and funerals shared with relatives and neighbors, in Tapp City she dwelt among strangers, floating derelict on a sea of silence.

None of them, Mama, Papa nor Addie, had made many acquaintances among Tapp City people. Their speech and their habits marked them too plainly as belonging elsewhere. In the end it was easier to keep to each other.

*

While she was thinking of her parents, the boy with the hot dog had been replaced by two teenaged girls in short skirts. They had great masses of frizzled hair, rounded bare arms, and firm, rosy thighs. The one with striped socks looked to be a few years older than the one wearing a necklace of green beads. Their faces bore a distinct family resemblance. As Addie watched them, they began kicking at one another's feet.

"I'm going to lie under the sun-lamp this afternoon," said Beads. "Look how white I am."

"Look how brown *I* am," said Stripes.

They giggled, still kicking.

"Tie my shoe," said Stripes.

"Better say *my* shoe on *your* foot," said Beads.

"I was going to wear your black jeans, but I thought you'd be mad."

"Don't wear *any* of my jeans."

"Tomorrow," said Stripes, "we go to the dentist to have our cavities filled."

"*I* don't get cavities," said Beads. "*You* get cavities."

Again, they giggled.

Listening, Addie felt their talk was like a song sung in two parts, point and counterpoint. It rose, intertwining, out of their shared lives. It bubbled from them like a bright spring until Addie found she couldn't imagine one girl without the other. They defined one another in spurts of calculated humor like a vaudeville act.

How lovely to have a sister, Addie thought. To whisper secrets under the bed covers. To comb out one another's hair. Later on, to share memories of parents and childhood. Even after parents passed on, to be yet in company with people of your own blood.

Addie had often pestered Mama to give her a sister or brother. She'd kept it up even when they were living in the house on Valhalla Drive. What Mama told Addie was this: "I'd think it a sin to birth another babe into this meaningless puzzle of a world!" There was another, hidden, reason as well.

Of a sudden the sister with the beads cried out, "Oh! Oh! Oh!" she said. "My necklace broke!"

Sure enough, green beads were bouncing everywhere over the floor.

"Better say *my* necklace on *your* neck," observed Stripes.

Giggling mightily, the two crawled about beneath the plastic seats gathering up green beads.

*

Addie closed her eyes and sniffed the appetizing smells from the snack bar just down the corridor. It was only mid-morning. Although, here in the airport, people were always eating. Any hour of the day you saw them with French fries. Pretzels. Sweet rolls. Frozen yogurt. Bagels. Crunching and munching.

How the human race enjoys eating! Addie thought. Even the most ordinary meals began in pleasant anticipation, moved through conviviality to gratification and ended in a shared contentment. *To be well fed is all some people asked of life.*

Downhome, Mama had loved to eat. However, in Tapp City, although she ate more, she ate quickly, snapping up her food without seeming to taste it. She appeared to eat for one purpose: to fuel her body. To stoke up energy needful for seeking out the answer to her eternal question.

*

Addie walked over and got in line at the snack bar. When her turn came, she asked for an orange drink.

"Open the cooler, granny," said the waitress. "No," she said, "to your right. See that lid? No, don't lift it. Slide it. Push sideways. Now that wasn't so hard, was it?"

Re-closing the cooler, Addie wondered at the trouble she'd had in her lifelong dealing with objects. And more especially with people. She supposed it had to do with being the child of parents who had difficulty communicating, even with one another.

As she paid for her drink and turned away, she came face to face with a lady wearing a wide-brimmed hat. The hat was made of straw and painted gold. The lady's earrings were clusters of silver acorns. The effect of the gold and silver colors against the lady's ebony skin was breathtakingly beautiful.

All humankind had dark skin to begin with, Addie thought, remembering the words of a book. Of a sudden she imagined herself all over a lovely duskiness.

"My blood pressure measured 118 over 60," the lady in the gold hat told her companion.

"It's plain you ain't worrying yourself over *any*thing," the companion said.

"You can bank that, honey," replied the lady. Throwing her head back, she gave a great laugh. All the little acorns jingled.

*

Mama's blood pressure had increased as she put on weight, but she'd refused to take medicine for it. If she'd been in Colerain County, Mama said, she'd have known which herbs to gather and what brew to brew. Here in the city, she mistrusted both the doctors and the drugs they prescribed.

Of course, she'd wasted away somewhat toward the end, but Addie remembered her best as a buxom woman. Big-hipped. Heavy-faced. High-colored and more or less ferocious in her manner. She seemed to be continually impatient with all that lay around her.

Cracking nuts for cakes, how smartly she'd brought down the hammer, sending pieces of shell flying, often smashing the kernels to useless mush as well. She'd dusted the furniture with quick, impulsive movements, cracking ashtrays and up-ending vases. Cooking at the stove, she was likely to grab at skillets and pots so as to burn her fingers or the fleshy underparts of her arms. In her flipping and flopping, Addie thought, Mama had resembled a fish on a riverbank. Like a fish she'd seemed to exist in the wrong element.

Mama was a woman who took up causes. Although none of them seemed to satisfy her for long. It was as if she sucked each one dry, then dropped it and took up another. She read books in the same way. Rarely did she finish one book before starting the next.

The longer Mama failed to make the world yield up its enigma, the more mistrustful she grew of having any converse with it at all. In the end all written knowledge struck her as unsound. But although she stopped reading books, she never stopped asking her question.

During Mama's last illness, Addie sat by her bed. Every now and again, Mama raised herself onto her elbows.

"What was the point?" Mama asked her.

The last time she raised herself, instead of words, blood bubbled out between her lips. Addie found it somehow less frightening than the question.

When her own time came, Addie felt she'd be more glad than sorry, tired as she was of the fruitless task Mama'd set her.

*

While she ate her sandwich and drank her orange pop, Addie listened to a conversation about gum trees.

"I wanted a red oak," explained a man on the seat behind her. "You know, the kind that keeps its leaves all winter. But *she* wanted a gum tree. So, of course, we bought a gum tree. We planted it beside the front porch."

"And did it thrive?" asked his friend.

"It did indeed. But the marriage didn't. Now every autumn I call down a curse on her head while raking up those goddamned leaves and seed pods."

*

When they first came to Tapp City, Papa'd brought with him a slip off the lilac bush that grew beside their cabin. He planted it at the back of his garden where it still flourished. Thinking how, each spring, the air filled with perfume from its pale lavender flowerets, of a sudden Addie knew she'd be sorry, after all, to leave the earth. The astronauts, too, she thought, must be saddened to see its round ball sink away, even though they knew they would soon return to it.

Of themselves, her fingers gripped onto the arms of the red plastic chair. *Suppose God came this minute to take me,* she told herself. *He'd have a hard time prying me loose!* Then she let go of the chair, feeling foolish to have entertained such a notion.

*

In the Ladies', Addie had to turn sideways to maneuver her valise into the stall. Once she'd got it in, she hung it from a hook so that, while she did her business, she sat staring at the purple embroidery. Before starting, of course, she carefully covered the toilet seat with tissue as Mama had taught her. Down among the hills each farm had its outhouse with round holes where only the family sat. Here in the city, you settled where anyone might have perched before you.

In the next stall Addie heard a mother speaking with her little daughter.

"Now, Susie," she said. "Won't you? For Mommy?"

"No!" said Susie.

Addie admired Susie's spunk. But of course, as they always do, the mother won out in the end.

Before she left the stall, Addie read the several messages scratched in the green paint above the tissue dispenser. "Let's boogie!" "Lonesome and blue." "Mercedes Benz." "I love him but he doesn't love me," and "Born to twirl." In pencil on the opposite wall were two sentences, both written by the same hand. "Who are you?" said one. "Who am I?" said the other.

When Addie stepped up to a basin to wash her hands, the water switched off prematurely and she had to keep turning it back on. The woman next to her was doing the same. She was holding something under the faucet.

"I always have to rinse my plate," said the woman. "Them tomater seeds gets underneath." She turned the water on. And Addie turned it on. They smiled at one another with a sudden sense of intimacy.

*

Outside the Ladies', for the shortest of moments, Addie seemed to detect, on certain nearby faces, an expression she couldn't name. Further, she sensed an odd, stretched quality to the air. A delicate tightness akin to the surface of a soap bubble. Almost as soon as she noticed it, however, the strangeness relaxed its hold. Dissolved away. Most likely, Addie supposed, it hadn't been there at all.

Near the girl collecting boarding passes, people were hugging and kissing. Weeping and wailing. Biding tearful goodbyes. Meanwhile, in the long corridor that led in from the landing planes, there was also kissing and hugging but less of wailing. More of smiles. An abundance of welcomings.

Watching these travelers, Addie thought how much people look like other people. For she could readily pick out men and women who resembled certain of her past bosses, or who simulated former fellow-workers, or even Mama and Papa so that, of a sudden, this thought came to her: *When people leave you, why not switch your caring to their look-alikes? It would give you such release from grief.*

Everyone had look-alikes. For instance, the slight, dark-skinned boy across the room was the image of Heber Kilkinney who, in the fifth grade downhome, had presented her with a yellow cat's eye marble. The next spring, as petals dropped onto their shoulders like tinted snow, he'd kissed her under the plum tree on Fowler's Mountain. Afterward, many a night that summer, she'd seen him standing in the yard grass staring up at her bedroom window, the light from the moon resting on his wild black hair.

However, as the boy across the room turned toward her, she saw that, after all, he didn't resemble Heber Kilkinney all that much. Besides which, of course, she knew *If Heber were still alive, he'd be, not a boy, but an old, old man. This boy was alien, the same as all the other people in the airport. The deepest significance of his life, like theirs, was submerged in silence and therefore unknown. And after all,* she thought, *a body can't actually give her used love to strangers like second-hand clothes. It can't be done.*

Of a sudden Addie was overcome by a feeling of hopelessness. For what a puzzle it was after all: life, with its multiplicity and its complexity! And to expect an aged spinster to tease out even a modicum of meaning in it all was beyond possibility.

*

After she'd walked about for some time, Addie found herself beside a large window overlooking the runways. Bits of fine snow had begun to slant down. Overhead a plane lifted into flight, its engines making the roar of a whirlwind. Addie held her breath but no Voice spoke to her out of it, as one had spoken to Job. Instead, what she heard was the remark of one airline stewardess to another as they walked past: "When Joey started taking me out, all he wanted was beer and all I wanted was tequila."

How sorry that was, judged against what she had hoped to hear from God but how it tickled her! Addie lifted up the valise and smiled, unseen, into its purple threads.

Both funny and sad, this scrap of conversation in the way certain old letters at Valhalla Drive were both silly and sad. Through the years these letters had laid in the cedar chest done up in packets tied with ribbon. Addie read them only after Mama was gone: faded words spidering across brittle paper, red two-cent stamps on the envelopes. They were from Mama's girl friends and boy friends of long ago.

These young people sent one another verses. Collected them. Demanded them. Pleaded for them. Copied and savored them. And passed them on. Who could take such doggerel seriously? Nobody. Yet Addie'd read them over until they must have lodged in the secret places of her brain because out they tumbled when she least expected them.

"Round is the ring that has no end
So is my love for you, my friend."

"Drink your coffee, drink your tea
Go to heaven and think of me."

"My love for you will never fail
As long as pussy has a tail."

"Snow on the Mountain
Sun can't melt it
I love you
And I can't help it."

"Remember O remember me,
Though many miles apart we be."

"Apples are good
Peaches are better
If you love me
Answer my letter."

"My pen is dim,
My ink is pale,
But my love for you
Will never fail."

So much poetry made Addie feel flushed and over-excited. She closed her eyes and leaned her face on the window-pane, savoring the feel of the cool glass against her forehead.

"Write me a letter," Heber Kilkinney had said the day she left Colerain. But, although she'd tried, the words wouldn't come. In the end she'd given up the attempt. He had exited her life as the space craft must have, by now, exited the earth. He had disappeared beyond her sight. Beyond her hearing. Almost beyond her remembering. Her fault, surely. *Do we, then, bring isolation on ourselves,* she wondered, while blaming it on chance? Or on others? Or, even, on geography?

A shaft of sunlight, straying through the window, rested on her head like a warm, absolving hand. When she opened her eyes, she saw the people in the waiting room, reflected in the glass, floating together as in a clear sea.

Sitting with her back to the windows, her specs on her lap, Addie's chin dipped as she fell into a doze. She woke just in time to save her glasses from tumbling onto the floor. When she put them on, what came more or less into focus was a lady in a red dress. The silken material clung to her thighs, fell low at her bosom and ended two inches above her knees. Her lips, moist and pouting, were painted the red of her dress, and she carried a red silk purse. The look in her eyes was devil-may-care.

Addie recalled that she had seen such a look before. Seen it, of all places in the cedar chest on Valhalla Drive, amongst the old letters. It was in a black-and-white snapshot of Mama in a summer dress, balancing herself on the wing of an airplane.

There she stood, thin and reckless, reaching both arms above her head and, although this plane was on the ground, Addie understood that Mama'd had a wish to wing-walk in the sky. That she'd wanted adventurous days. And wild nights.

The truth was that, as a girl, Mama had longed for a virile husband, for an abundance of rough-and-tumble love-making. For many baby-mouths tugging at her breasts, one following the other down the years. All this was in her eyes. It was in the bold look she turned on the camera which, Addie thought, *must* have been held by one of her beaux.

Sadly, who Mama got for a husband was Papa, a man ultimately obsessed with the postal system. The power that should have flowed to his genitals rose instead into his brain where it fixated on philately. On postal rules and regulations.

Mama's and Papa's sex life, Addie surmised, having started as not much, progressed to next to nothing when Papa began to spend his meager energy writing a book, a comprehensive history of the postal service.

When he wasn't working on his manuscript, he was talking about it. During her formative years, Addie learned many facts and figures, lists and milestones concerned with communication. She soon knew that the first messages, oral, then written, were carried by runners given fixed stations where they held themselves in readiness to receive a notice and carry it to the next point. That the Incas had such a system 700 years ago. That the Persians under Cyrus, the Holy Roman Empire, and Medieval Europe developed courier services.

That a postal system was organized by the Hanse Towns of Northern Germany in the 12th century, by the University of Paris in the 13th century, and by Great Britain in the 14th century. That the first adhesive stamp, carrying a portrait of Queen Victoria, was issued in 1840.

Semi-forgotten fragments of postal knowledge yet flew about Addie's brain as if her head were full of bats. The first post office were opened in the United States in 1639. Alexander Hamilton was the first post master general. Mail was carried over a system of Post roads, one of which ran from New York to Boston. Overland mail reached California from Missouri by stagecoach. The first perforated stamps were issued in 1854. Mail boxes, 1855. The Pony Express traveled to the west coast in 1860. Rural Free Delivery, 1896. Parcel post, 1913. Air mail, 1918.

At some point in the writing of his book, Addie felt that Papa had ceased to care for Mama. Or for Addie herself. Ceased even to care for God. In the end, Papa cared only for the postal service.

*

A thin, whooping siren sounded. Addie looked around in time to see a motorized cart, driven by a uniformed employee, proceed down the room carrying four disabled people and their luggage. The people were pale and ill-looking. They stared ahead with expressionless faces.

Shadow people, thought Addie, and images of Charon and the Styx rose before her mind's eye. For a moment she felt shaken as if she herself were on the cart traveling toward some final darkness.

"Shadow people" was, of course, what Mama had named Papa and Addie. "The shadow man and the shadow woman." This was after Papa had stopped writing his book. When he had even stopped talking about it but only sat in his chair staring through the front windows. Addie, too, had always been a watcher, not a doer. A listener not a communicant. "A wallflower at life's dance," was how Mama described her.

Addie understood that this judgment contained an element of truth. Yet, in her mind, she quarreled with it. She reasoned that if her task, imposed by Mama herself, was to discover the figure of the dance, she had much better study it from a distance than caught up in the pattern. However, she never said such to Mama who was impatient of metaphors.

A chunky, dark-skinned Hispanic-looking woman wearing corduroy pants and a long black T-shirt threaded her way through the airport patrons carrying an incredibly massive musical instrument. As Addie watched she turned and placed it into the arms of her companion, a young girl in a filmy ballet-length skirt and an off-the-shoulder peasant blouse.

The woman's face showed no makeup. She wore her hair twisted into a knot on the back of her head. The girl's face, on the other hand, was tinted, eye, cheek and lip, as exquisitely as a China doll's. After a time, the girl handed the instrument back to the woman so that it became impossible to decide which of the two was its owner.

Addie tried to guess what kind of instrument it might be. A small harp? A bass viol? A tuba? Its true shape was hidden inside a rigid case exhibiting many planes, curves and bulges. The combination of case and instrument appeared to be distressingly heavy.

The two women were, in some ways, as mysterious as the instrument. They seemed not to belong together. Their looks and manner were so remarkably incongruous that it seemed unlikely they were mother and daughter. Or even teacher and pupil. They appeared to be of differing social classes, of disparate neighborhoods, probably even from different ethnic groups. The only link between them appeared to be the enigmatic instrument.

As the two women passed close before her, Addie shrank back instinctively. *Suppose they were gangsters' molls. Suppose the case contained tommyguns?* Truth to tell, there were mysteries better left unsolved. Although Mama wouldn't have thought so. Nor Papa.

Take the matter of birds. Early in his life, Papa had wished to know the name of every bird he saw. Along with its habits. He bought a book and a pair of binoculars and went about spying on them, making lists.

Mama, for her part, puzzled over the meaning of birds in the Bible. She read out to Addie what the Bible had to say about them. "The birds of the air have nests but the Son of man hath not where to lay his head," read Mama. "Mine heritage is unto me as a speckled bird and the birds round about are against her," and "The time of the singing of birds is come." "What does this mean?" asked Mama after every passage and of course Addie couldn't say. Although the speckled bird was clear enough. At least to a body from the hills living in the flatlands.

One summer they'd visited a beach where what seemed to be a thousand sea gulls sat together on the sand. Addie, not more than three, wearing a little red swimsuit, had broken away from Mama and run in amongst the gulls. To this day she could feel the strong gusts from their wings as they rose about her. Watching them lift off by the 20s, by the 50s, she had wanted neither to name them nor interpret them but to be one of them. To do as they did. She had yearned to rise up and challenge the sky.

*

Feeling weak, Addie fished the Granny Smith apple out of her valise and ate it while watching three soldiers play rummy on top of a duffel bag. They were neatly dressed in olive drab with leather boots and small caps. A man of about sixty stood close by watching the cards fall.

"In 1946 I crossed the country in a troop train," he told them. "We filled our mess kits with stew the cooks made in big steel drums over open fires."

"Army chow hasn't changed much," the soldiers said and laughed. One of them spread out a run of hearts.

"We trained in sight of Mt. Rainier," the older man said. "Every day it poured. We marched all day with full field packs. I never got a day of leave. I always got gigged. Either my rifle had dust in it or my blanket wasn't tucked up tight enough."

"Soldiering is hell," said the boy with the run of hearts and winked at his two friends.

"You may say so," agreed the old man. "We crossed to Japan in a hurricane. The ship spun like it was going down a drain. Two men were swept overboard and drowned."

One of the soldiers laid down all his cards. "Gin," he said. The other two groaned.

*

Addie's uncles, Mama's brothers, who fought in the Kaiser's War, saw action in the Argon Forest and come home with medals pinned to their chests. Every year the three of them marched in the Decoration Day parade at Sardis carrying muskets on their shoulders.

"Men has all the adventures," Mama said. All her life she envied her brothers their war. With most of the young men from Colerain gone over the ocean, only Papa, blind without his specs, was left and he and Mama fell in together. They'd been courting for the better part of a year by the time of the armistice.

When all the boys came home, some coughing from mustard gas, some missing an arm or leg, Addie supposed Papa had seemed vigorous and whole by comparison. Her parents were married the following spring.

*

Addie nibbled the core of the Granny Smith. Eve shared her apple and rested the sin in Adam. Addie'd eaten hers every bit herself. Feeling ennobled by this thought, she stiffened in her purpose. Supposing life had a point, she'd, sooner or later, spy it out. *And if God disapproves,* she thought, *let the blame fall on me alone. Let Mama be left out of it.* Because, if the truth were known, Addie sometimes suspected God, like Addie herself, had secrets He'd as leave no one poked into.

For some time, Addie had been aware of groups of people standing about together, whispering. Straining to hear, she saw a silver balloon float up to rest against a corner of the ceiling high above the ticket counter for USAir. Around it, all but veiling it from sight, hung the flags of all the nations.

That will never be got down, thought Addie, and she looked about for a crying child. Instead, she saw an elderly woman whose right arm was done up in plaster and thrust out at an awkward angle from her body. This plastered arm was supported in a canvas sling.

Every now and again the woman took the arm out of the sling and stretched it up into the air. *Her doctor has told her to do this*, Addie supposed. And she thought, *Poor woman! How does she comb her hair?* But in fact, the woman's hair was cut so short as to need very little combing. It was chopped off, in an unbecoming way, level with her earlobes.

Addie pictured the woman having her hair shampooed, then trimmed in a beauty parlor, her arm sticking up into the air the while. However, this seemed unlikely. The woman had a threadbare look. *Perhaps*, thought Addie, a *relative cut it as she and her parents had used to crop one another's hair to save the price of a barber.*

A man sat next to the injured woman, reading a travel magazine.

"And the bathroom mirror's too high," the woman told him, seemingly adding another to a series of complaints. "I can't see myself in it. The kitchen cupboards is too. I can't reach them." In truth she was a short little body, scarcely bigger than a minute. What there was of her was exceedingly gnarled and bent.

The man nodded, turning a page.

"The wind blows through cracks around the door. And we ain't allowed pets. I gave Kitty to people as lives in the country and I ain't seen her since. When I find somebody that'll drive me out to visit her, she hides in the mow.

"The man in the unit beside me, he wrote to Washington and they let him keep his old dog. Well, last week I was out on the front pavement trying to get some air, using my walker so as not to fall, and here comes Mrs. Davies, the Super, and ordered me inside. Said the noise of my walker was disturbing others. It was making that old dog bark, you see."

"You can't win, Aunt Lil," said the man, studying a photo of Bangkok.

"Last Saturday evening," said Lil, "Thelma and Glenn came to visit me. They was telling me about their trip to Alaska when Mrs. Davies knocked on the door. 'No visitors after 10:30 P.M.,' she says. So Thelma and Glenn had to leave. It was so interesting, too."

"They'll be back," Lil's nephew said.

"You remember that county health person?" Lil asked. "The one as comes onct a week and washes my clothes and helps me into the bathtub? Well, somebody seen me up to the P.O. last Monday and that night Mrs. Davies told me I couldn't have help unless I was housebound."

"You'll be housebound now your arm's broke," the man said.

Once Mama broke her collarbone. This was shortly before her stroke. She'd been dizzy off and on all that morning. Her eyesight seemed somehow blurred. So pretty soon down she went onto the cement floor in the basement at Valhalla Drive.

That time Addie insisted on a doctor. But directly they got home from the doctor's office, Mama ripped off the bandage he'd tied on her. She said it smelled funny. So Addie bound her up in an old scarf instead. A white one with tassels. She wore it for several weeks knotted around her neck.

"If you had one of them leather caps," Addie'd told her, "you'd look for all the world like a old-time airplane pilot." It was true. To her dying day, Mama'd kept that devil-may-care wing-walker look in her eyes.

One of the airport employees took Lil by the unbroken arm and helped her across the floor and into the mechanized cart while her relative gathered up her bags and boxes and loaded them in beside her. Then off she went, the siren sounding, Whoop! Whoop! warning everyone to get out of her way.

Addie picked up her valise and, hiding her face behind it, smiled in secret to see Little Bit ride off so grand.

The terminal was moderately chilly. Addie buttoned her coat. Outside snow was falling, streaking across the windows as if white lines were being marked on the air by an invisible hand. Indistinct voices buzzed around her so that she felt like a bee in a hive.

"Keep your luggage and personal belongings with you at all times," airport security boomed out. The amplified voice had a badgering tone that put Addie in mind of Lil's Super, Mrs. Davies.

Now and again, Addie thought, that directive made a body want to stomp off and leave their suitcase sitting in the middle of the floor just for spite.

Of course, security hadn't *always* said such things. The fact was that two months ago in the airport, a man had been caught concealing a pipe bomb under the shirts in his carry-on. When the newspapers wrote up the incident, ticket sales for all the airlines dropped. Addie understood that airport security was simply seeking to preserve life. And also, of course, the economic health of the airlines. *People who bossed other people generally had good motives*, Addie supposed. *Although sometimes, as in the case of Mrs. Davies, they only thought they had.*

*

Sitting the next row over, Addie spotted a man with the largest nose she'd ever seen, bar none. *If this man were to step outdoors on a sunny day*, Addie told herself, *his nose would not only shade his mouth and chin but his belt-buckle as well and even, possibly, the laces of his shoes. Think of that.*

He was shaven and clipped, and most elegantly got up in pale blue shirt, regimental tie and gray suit with vest. Addie saw the pink dome of his head peeping through the top-most strands of his fine colorless hair as he bowed his head over his drawn-up knees. He looked at no one but exclusively down into his lap where a small computer lay outspread. Beside him stood a natty briefcase in maroon leather, unzipped, from which papers poked, riotously. Contracts, guessed Addie. Reports. Assorted print-outs along with a copy of the *Wall Street Journal.*

Observing the big-nosed man, Addie mused that if certain people resemble other people, so do certain acts resemble other acts.

From a certain angle, this man appeared to have a table before him whereon, in his sartorial splendor, he seemed to feast like the honored guest at a banquet.

"Go you up to the feast," Mama had read to Addie from the Bible. "I go not up yet unto this feast," she'd read, "for my time is not yet full come." Listening to these words, Addie had suspected that Mama secretly believed the point of life would turn out to be a sort of harvest dinner in heaven where all the people who had lived on earth, city people and country people, would sit around having an endless chat.

Like Papa's postal facts, Mama's scripture readings were forever swooping about Addie's brain. Sometimes, like wind-blown bits of paper, they stuck for a time to this person or that event before dropping away.

Big Nose, absorbed in his calculations, consulted a manual from his briefcase, then went on picking at the keys. After some time, an airport employee approached him.

"You dropped your boarding pass, sir," said the employee, "in the Gents."

Big Nose took hold of the pass so that, for a moment, the two men were joined by the piece of red plastic. In that instant they grinned, each one at the other. Then the airport employee let go, Big Nose tucked the pass into the inside pocket of his suit coat, and the two parted.

"Thank you," Big Nose said, his voice sounding somewhat like a rusty gate-hinge, turning.

*

Papa's voice was low and sweet as a breeze rustling through sassafras. "Voices are only one of our many modes of communication," Papa'd told her. "Each of us comes into this world with a message. Some are delivered. Some are not."

"The transfer of feelings, thoughts and information from person to person, underlies all human cooperation and has an importance which can scarcely be exaggerated." This was the opening sentence of Papa's book about the Postal Service. Except when describing this book, Papa was brief-spoken to a fault throughout his life. Toward its end he fell into silence as a pebble drops into the sea. What his final thoughts were, Addie had no way of knowing. However, she often speculated about them.

This is what she imagined: Picture a scoffer on his death bed. He closes his eyes and breathes his last prepared for what? A void? Pure nothingness? Instead, he sees: angels.

Who could say with any confidence that such things do not occur? No one. Addie believed it had happened to her father. The more so because, just at the end, she saw his lips begin to move and so felt certain he was naming them to himself as he'd named the birds: "Cherubim. Seraphim. Thrones. Dominions. Virtues. Principalities. Powers."

Addie, valise in hand, descended the stairs into the basement. Newly arrived passengers were gathered around the luggage carousels of the various airlines.

She watched now one, now another person lunge with a sort of frantic abandon and snatch at a bag as it humped and jolted past. It was like watching people bobbing for apples. Or gigging frogs.

Some timid souls, mostly older women, made their attempt too late, then stood in dismay as their bag disappeared into the nether regions. After a long wait, here it came again, so that, like it or not, they must make another try. Another valiant effort.

As the newly disembarked passengers were various, so was the baggage. There were cases, large and small, with hard shells in jewel colors. There were soft canvas rolls, backpacks, matched sets of luggage, and orphan suitcases in peeling leather tied up with lengths of rope. All shapes and sizes of boxes and pokes rode around and around, each one lumpy and strained by its inner contents. Once in a great while one of these gave up the ghost and burst, spewing garments and toilette articles over the carousel like popping corn.

Addie visited three carousels. On approaching the fourth, she beheld a great deal of activity all on the part of one plumpish young man. Now he dived at the carousel, now he leaped back clutching a bag for all the world, thought Addie, like a seagull snapping up fish. Yet none of them were *his* bags. For he presented his catches to this person or that, all the while bowing and nodding.

"Here's yours," he said. "And here's yours."

People received their luggage from his hands with surprise colored by suspicion. Soon, however, they were nodding and bowing, too. "Many thanks," the people said. "Many, many thanks!"

At the last, the man caught up what appeared to be his own bags, lifted them from the turn-around, and carried them to the place his family waited for him.

There was a squat, fair-haired woman Addie took to be his wife and a number of children of assorted sizes. There was also an elderly lady standing somewhat apart. She had drawn herself up into a stiff and dignified pose, the while leaning on a heavy cane made of dark wood.

"Now, Grandam, take my arm," said the young man hustling up to her. "And you, Bridget, you take the other. Up the stairs we all go! I will return for the luggage."

And off they all went, father, mother, children and granny, the father talking volubly now to his family now to others, shouting out to people they passed, wishing them good-day, giving them directions and advice, begging them for the answer to this or that question about their travel plans, about their lives outside the airport.

As for Addie, she trailed along behind the young man's entourage, feeling as if she were bringing up the rear of a parade.

On the floor above, the young man guided his ladies toward chairs. "Sit! Sit!" he told them. "Grandam, rest. Bridget, rest. I will bring tea. Big cups of strong black tea!" Then off he trotted in the midst of his children, his hips, his considerable paunch commencing to rock to and fro as he gained momentum.

This, said Addie to herself, *is not a watcher but a do-er. Not only a listener but a talker. A determined communicant. One who won't allow being different to stop his communicating.* For he seemed to be foreign. He spoke with an accent. Middle European. Or Scandinavian. Addie had no ear for languages.

Very soon here he came again bearing the promised Styrofoam cups of tea. The children were consuming popsicles of various colors. The Communicant himself was eating a purple one.

As he handed down the tea, two women wandered past turning their heads this way and that, staring about uncertainly.

"Are you looking for it?" the Communicant cried out to them. "It is down that way," he informed them. "Just past the rubber tree plant. You cannot see the sign until you get closer."

He means the Ladies', Addie surmised, *but is too delicate to name it.* And she lifted the valise to her face, giggling silently against the embroidery.

The Communicant disappeared again, this time alone, to return almost at once with the luggage. He bustled about piling it on a cart, straightening and arranging the bags and cases.

"I have called a taxi, Bridget," said the Communicant. "I have called a taxi, Grandam. Soon we shall drive home."

He sat down panting and scrubbed the purple from his lips with a crumpled handkerchief. As he scrubbed, he turned eagerly to the older woman, swiveling his chunky body in the too-small seat, trying to see into her face.

"Did you like the Revival, Grandam?" he asked her. "It moved one, didn't it? The preaching was inspirational, eh?"

The old lady, sitting ramrod straight, with her cane upright between her knees, spoke in a slow, deep voice. "Not like in the old country," was what she said. *It was the same with Mama,* Addie thought. Her mother had always felt certain she'd left God sitting on a mountaintop down in the Appalachian hills, too far off to be of any practical use.

Papa also put little credence in the Tapp City churches, although he now and again muttered hymns while clipping the grass or painting the porches on Valhalla Drive. "Bringing in the sheaves," sang Papa, and, "Help of the helpless O abide with me." He did so with an edge of sarcasm to his voice. Papa's religion was the postal service.

In *his* mind there'd been no doubt as to the point of life: it was communication. He believed in it but couldn't do it. No more could Addie. This was an inherited defect, she supposed, like six toes or a cleft pallet. Only more hidden. More difficult to modify.

Of a sudden Addie recalled the fish she'd seen in the optometrist's office. This, she supposed, was the nearest she'd ever come to a mystical revelation. And it was suspect since it had to do with eye-drops.

But it also had to do with the optometrist's fingers touching her face, a unique experience, and with his repeated question. "Is this better or is that better?" he'd said, seeming to hang on each of her answers. Communication, she suspected, had more to do with both physical contact and the spoken word than Papa would ever allow.

During their long life together, why hadn't Mama taken a lover? Addie'd often wondered but never asked. Papa would have been relieved, she thought. Eased of the constant pressure to do what he couldn't or wouldn't do. And Mama might have found her perennial question finally satisfied.

Because sometimes Addie suspicioned that Mama hadn't intended to demand, "What is the point of life?" so much as to ask the less grand, "What is the point of *my* life?" And that the point she'd wished it to have was sexual.

All her days, Mama had reached out to Papa and to God. Neither of them had responded. At least not in the way she'd expected. Or needed.

*

Now that she was sitting with her back to the windows, Addie once again looked out over the several television sets scattered about the terminal, some on tables, some in alcoves, others fastened high on walls. Crowds were yet bunched about them. *What sort of images,* Addie pondered, *could pull people to them, could hold people in front of them in this manner?*

Picking up Mama's valise, she crossed the floor toward the closest set. As she drew near, she realized that, in fact, an identical picture was on every screen, that the same event was being shown over and over, and at that this had been going on for a comparatively long time.

Peering past heads and over shoulders, Addie made out, on every set, a feathery billowing somewhat in the shape of a seagull with, at the top, two projections like wings.

For the briefest of moments, she wondered: *Could this be the materialization of an archangel?*

She set down the valise, removed her specs and rubbed her eyes. After she'd wiped the lenses on her sleeve, she moved closer and, replacing her glasses, strove mightily to make sense of the image. It seemed to have become woolly and elongated. At the apex were reaching fingers.

And now she noticed that the people around the TV sets were weeping. Tears ran down their faces as they gripped one another's arms.

"No!" they said.

"This isn't real, is it?" someone asked.

"It didn't *explode* did it?" said someone else.

It was then that Addie understood that the image on the screens was the space vehicle. The one with the teacher in it. She understood that, earlier in the day, it had somehow blown apart and fallen from the sky.

All about her the weeping people embraced, murmuring their grief into one another's ears. And Addie wept, reaching out empty arms.

"Is that your bag, Missus?" A man in an airport security uniform was suddenly speaking into her right ear. "Did you just now walk away from that bag?" he asked her, pointing his finger behind her with a jabbing motion. Another uniformed man came to stand beside the first.

Addie glanced over her shoulder. There indeed sat Mama's purple valise alone in the middle of the floor like an abandoned puppy. Almost, it seemed to be whimpering.

"There's not one thing in it." Addie said.

However, the two security guards hurried her onto a motorized cart. As they drove her slowly off across the floor to the accompaniment of short, wordless whoops, Addie strained to look back at the TV screens where the space craft kept rising and exploding until the repeated image seemed not so much to show the destruction of the vehicle as to praise the valiant, the determined, the unceasing effort of the launch.

Photo by Greg Reese

Annabel Thomas was born in Columbus, Ohio, and graduated from The Ohio State University. She worked as a reporter and feature writer for *The Columbus Citizen*, a morning newspaper. She also taught grade school and for many years helped her husband, a veterinarian, treat large and small animals. She has four children and lives in Columbus.

Her parents were born and raised in the Appalachian Mountains of Southeast Ohio, and she returned there each summer so that the mountains and the people had a strong influence on her writing. "Probably because the hill country exists for me largely in their remembrances," she says, "it has turned, in my brain, into myth and symbol, the stuff of which my poems and stories are made. I believe the pull of different cultures resulted in a sort of double vision, a feeling of standing outside my own times, looking on from a distance. I feel this tension at the heart of my fiction."

The Phototropic Woman, her first story collection, won the Iowa School of Letters Short Fiction Award in 1981 and was published by University of Iowa Press. A second volume of short fiction, *Knucklebones*, won the Willa Cather Award in 1994 and was published in 1995 by Helicon Nine Editions in Kansas City, MO. Two novels, *Blood Feud* (1998) and *Stone Man Mountain* (2002) were published by University of Tennessee Press. Her *A Well of Living Water*, novella appeared in *Human Anatomy: Three Fictions* from Bottom Dog Press in 1993.

Bottom Dog Press
Appalachian Writing Series

Choices: Three Novella by Annabel Thomas, $18

Pottery Town Blues : Stories by Karen Kotrba $16

Labor Days/Labor Nights, by Larry D. Thacker $18

The Country Doctor's Wife, by Cornelia Cattell Thompson, $18

The Long Way Home, Ron Lands, $18

Mingo Town & Memories, Larry Smith, $15

40 Patchtown: A Novel, Damian Dressick, $18

Mama's Song, P. Shaun Neal, $18

Fissures and Other Stories, by Timothy Dodd, $18

Old Brown, by Craig Paulenich, $16

A Wounded Snake: A Novel, by Joseph G. Anthony, $18

Brown Bottle: A Novel, by Sheldon Lee Compton, $18

Small Room with Trouble on My Mind, by Michael Henson, $18

Drone String: Poems, by Sherry Cook Stanforth, $16

Voices from the Appalachian Coalfields, by Mike & Ruth Yarrow,$17

Wanted: Good Family, by Joseph G. Anthony, $18

Sky Under the Roof: Poems, by Hilda Downer, $16

Green-Silver and Silent: Poems, by Marc Harshman, $16

The Homegoing: A Novel, by Michael Olin-Hitt, $18

She Who Is Like a Mare: by Karen Kotrba, $16

Smoke: Poems, by Jeanne Bryner, $16

Broken Collar: A Novel, by Ron Mitchell, $18

Pattern Maker's Daughter: Poems, by Sandee Gertz Umbach, $16

The Free Farm: A Novel, by Larry Smith, $18

Sinners of Sanction County: Stories, by Charles Dodd White, $17

Learning How: Stories, Yarns & Tales, by Richard Hague, $18

The Long River Home: A Novel, by Larry Smith, $16

Appalachian Writing Series Anthologies

Unbroken Circle: Stories of Cultural Diversity in the South,
Eds. Julia Watts and Larry Smith, $18

Appalachia Now: Short Stories of Contemporary Appalachia,
Eds. Charles Dodd White and Larry Smith, $18

Degrees of Elevation: Short Stories of Contemporary Appalachia,
Eds. Charles Dodd White and Page Seay, $18

Free Shipping. http://smithdocs.net